ELIZABETH GAGE

the hourglass

MIRA® BOOKS

*All the characters in this book have no existence outside the
imagination of the author, and have no relation whatsoever to
anyone bearing the same name or names. They are not even
distantly inspired by any individual known or unknown to the
author, and all the incidents are pure invention.*

*First published in Great Britain 2000
MIRA Books, Eton House, 18-24 Paradise Road,
Richmond, Surrey, TW9 1SR*

© J S L Productions, Inc. 1999

ISBN 1 55166 546 8

58-0008

*Printed and bound in Spain
by Litografía Rosés S.A., Barcelona*

To Maile

The past is a foreign country: they do things differently there.
—L. P. Hartley
The Go-Between

Some promises are not made to be kept. They express the fever of a brief convergence, the faith of a moment. They are all the more intense because they are doomed by time to transience, like the sudden crimson pattern etched in the clouds by a sun that has already set. Later we outgrow them because time forces us to do so. If we remember them—which we usually don't—it is with wistfulness, not disappointment. We look back on them indulgently, as vagaries of an earlier version of ourselves that we have overcome.

This is the story of a promise that shouldn't have been kept, but was kept. And of the strange consequences that occur when time is turned on its head.

It is fitting, then, that I should begin at the end.

Elizabeth Gage burst onto the commerical fiction scene with A GLIMPSE OF STOCKING which became a sensational *New York Times* bestseller. This novel was followed by PANDORA'S BOX, THE MASTER STROKE, TABOO and INTIMATE—all of which have enjoyed international success. Elizabeth Gage is married and has one daughter.

Also available from MIRA® Books and
Elizabeth Gage

CONFESSION

_____ Prologue _____

Some promises are not made to be kept. They express the fever of a brief convergence, the faith of a moment. They are all the more intense because they are doomed by time to transience, like the sudden crimson pattern etched in the clouds by a sun that has already set. Later we outgrow them because time forces us to do so. If we remember them—which we usually don't—it is with wistfulness, not disappointment. We look back on them indulgently, as vagaries of an earlier version of ourselves that we have overcome.

This is the story of a promise that shouldn't have been kept, but was kept. And of the strange consequences that occur when time is turned on its head.

It is fitting, then, that I should begin at the end. It was the day of my best friend's funeral. I had returned to the town of my youth to say goodbye to her. She was too young to die, and it seemed to me that her passing brought an end to much of what was worth hoping for in myself.

I felt nothing during the funeral or the graveside service. Only a deepening of loss which left me too empty for emotion itself. Perhaps this was because we had been so close. No one knew me as well as Lily. She was my earliest confidante and the person I identified with the most completely. Her stubborn refusal to let life defeat her had been an inspiration for me, because I was always less brave in seeking happiness than she was. In a way I must have feared that, if I allowed myself to feel her loss as it should be felt, I would follow her into the earth.

I expressed my sympathy to the surviving members of her family and to the many friends who had come to mourn her. I said fond goodbyes to those who knew me, packed up the few belongings I had brought on the trip with me and got in my car to leave town.

There were other graves to visit before I left—Lily was not my first loss—and I forced myself to visit them. Then I drove aimlessly along the old roads, stopping now and then to look at familiar places which had resisted the march of time and still looked much as they had looked when I was young here. I saw our school, and the park where we had played hopscotch and jump rope, and the drugstore where we drank our milk shakes and talked of boys.

I didn't get out of the car. The old places stayed behind the window, sliding past without touching me. There was a valedictory feeling in me for I was sure I would never see these sights again. But I felt no sadness; I was too drained for that. The most important thing about the past, I told myself a little complacently, is that it is gone.

As the afternoon waned I looked at my watch and realized it was time to take the county road out to the interstate and head home. But something held me back. I drove

around until dusk, noticing familiar lawns
and the sidewalks I used to take on foot or
on my bicycle. Then I went back to the
place where Lily and I had been closest as
girls.

It was a house overlooking the ocean,
with an enormous golf course arranged
around it like a garland. The place was
vastly changed. When we were little it had
been overgrown and unkempt. Now it had
been restored to its original splendor, which
dated from a time before we were born. It
seemed to me that these changes were like
layers of an archaeological site, insulating
me from my own past even more surely
than the mere passage of time.

I parked the car and walked past the
house to the golf course. I made my way
along fairways that were immaculately ton-
sured, the sound of briskly ticking lawn
sprinklers mingling with the song of the
crickets and the moody croak of a frog in
one of the water hazards.

I stopped at the fairway which had been
our special place. It had a lovely view of
the ocean, and I sat down on the grass to

enjoy it. The moon was rising shyly in the east. Its reflection shone on the waves like a stairway to the horizon.

I had seen this place in the colors of all the seasons, and also in the colors of my own changing perceptions as I grew up and felt things differently. This moon had risen over those waves, always the same, but bestowing itself on my eyes with different mysteries and different truths, according to the changes life had made in me.

I reflected that this place had played a recurrent, central role in my destiny. Everything important that had happened to me, it seemed, happened here, or was conceived here, or changed its course crucially here. The various threads of my life all intertwined in this spot. Here my greatest hopes had been born, and here the accidents that brought about the great joys and sorrows of my life.

And here my promises made—to the people I loved most, and to myself.

Still I did not allow my reflections to deepen into grief. Coldly as a geometrician, I admired the complexity of these convergences, and Lily's role in them. I told myself that if I wanted to say goodbye to everything about my past, to all hopes and all yearnings, I might as well say it here.

I turned toward the house, which I would have to pass in leaving. As I took my first step toward it, the moon glinted suddenly in one of its dark windows, as though to hold me back. And Lily's voice, to which I had turned deaf ears at the graveyard today, came to me for the first time.

At least let yourself remember, it said. *You owe me that.*

I hesitated. It was true. I did owe her that much of a farewell. But my emptiness was the only thing standing between me and a despair that might destroy the little I had left of myself.

"You ask too much," I said to the murmuring night. "I gave you everything I had when you were alive. I believed in you, I followed you, I even forgave you when you asked me to. Isn't that enough?"

Remember. The voice was intimate, powerful.

I might have resisted its summons, in

spite of everything, if another voice from my past had not come to join it.

Let's make this night last forever. The voice was Lily's, as it had sounded when she was a young girl. I turned to look at the fairway, where the words had originally been spoken. I was trembling.

If you want something badly enough, it will come true. This was a different voice, one I did not want to hear. It spoke with absolute conviction.

Then we'll be together forever. The words were my own, filled with a girlish yearning all the more eloquent for the fact that it had been buried so long.

The tears I had fought all day were coming fast now. The hovering moon seemed drowned by them. I shouldn't have come here, I thought. It was time to leave.

"I can't, Lily," I said. "It's too late. Everything is over now. It's no use."

Too late to refuse, said the voice. *You're remembering already.*

With a deep sigh I looked at the ocean that reared before me. A couple of late birds flew hurriedly across the dusky sky, calling loudly to each other, or perhaps to a third, which brought up the rear, following them as they disappeared behind the trees.

I surrendered. I realized that if the past is a thing we cannot recapture, it is also a thing we can never escape. Our self is conceived in it. The old roads remain imprinted on the aging feet that try to carry us away from them. The old hopes speak eloquently in our very despair. Indeed, I had already given in, when I took my first step toward this place. Lily was right.

"All right," I said, retracing my steps and sitting down in the cool grass. The moon shone brighter now, and the ocean whispered from beyond the lawns.

I took a deep breath, drying tears that would surely not be my last, and began to remember.

1

* * *

It is a beautiful day in early June, many years ago. We are standing in the sewing room of Lily's house. It is a modest house near the center of town, a couple of miles from the fancy places along the shore. Like most of the other local people, the Frances live in the shadow of the fine old county families whose forebears settled the Maine town two hundred years ago, and of the millionaires who discovered it in the last generation and built their mansions on the heights overlooking the ocean.

It is called Summer Harbor. In the summer it is home to wealthy tourists who come here to enjoy the crisp air, the chilly ocean and each other. For the rest of the year it is home to lobstermen, truck farmers, a few town residents who don't seem to do much of anything—and to me.

Lily's father runs a dry-goods business in town which was founded by his grandfather at the turn of the century. He likes to say he is "poor but happy," and he looks with amusement rather than envy at the huge shore places of the millionaires.

Outside the window the heavy green hills of late spring are visible. Beyond them, lending an odd breathlessness to the friendly sky, is the ocean. Inside the room there are several watercolor paintings on easels, one of which represents the view from the window. They were all done by Lily, whose talent attracted the attention of her art teacher in junior high school, and who uses this room as a makeshift studio in her spare time.

I turn to Lily. She is standing with

her arms held up while I stick pins in the seams of the dress she has on.

"Come on," she says. "My shoulders are killing me."

"Hang on another second."

I made the dress myself, from a pattern I saw in a fashion magazine. It would have been much too mature for anyone else her age, but Lily is tall and precociously shaped. She has always been slim, thanks to her youthful metabolism and terrific energy. But lately she has been having a growth spurt which has softened her tomboy shape. Her eyes are a burning blue, willful, impatient, beautiful when at rest.

"Okay," I say through the pins between my lips. "Now let's look."

She puts her arms down with a sigh and turns slightly to look at herself in the mirror.

"Oh, Kate!" she exclaims. "You're a wizard."

I am pleased. The dress is going to work out. Her breasts are just big enough to support the low-cut bodice.

Her bare shoulders look alert and pretty. The hemline shows off strong, shapely calves. It is a race against time, but her rapid growth allows her to make the dress her own.

She is thirteen years old. So am I.

"Do you think Jordan will like it?" she asks.

"Of course he'll like it," I say. "He has eyes, doesn't he? You look like a princess."

The metaphor seems particularly apt. Lily has always had a fresh naturalness that makes people like her— even those who might otherwise have been put off by her willful and slightly wild personality. But now adolescence is giving her the delicacy of a princess, the quiet sparkling desirability. The dress brings that out.

I glance at myself in the mirror and look quickly away. I am too ugly to look at. Lumpy, freckled, misshapen. If Lily is leaping gracefully into adolescence, I am caught at the clumsiest thirteen. My face is too wide, my limbs too heavy. Unlike my friend, I have only pimples to remind me of the new stage of life upon which I am embarking.

"You should come," Lily says. "Jordan will miss you."

I shake my head. "I don't want to come."

"Kate, don't be a poop!" she cries. "You've got to come! I can't be all alone with all those people I don't know. Say yes. Come on."

"No."

She turns back to the mirror. She realizes I am going to stick to my guns. There was a time when she would not have taken no for an answer. But she is growing up. I even sense the tact of an adult in her insistence that I come to the ball. She is making a show of insisting, because she doesn't want me to feel left out.

As I step back to look at the dress, I feel a familiar catch in my throat. Lily is everything I want to be, and never will be. This would make me unbearably jealous if I didn't feel so strongly that she is part of me. We have been best friends for so long that I have no real existence outside my closeness with her.

There is a knock at the door. Lily's younger brother, Eric, sticks his face into the room.

"Lily, Mom wants to see you," he says.

"What about?" Lily asks.

"Search me." Eric is a man of few words, and by far the least "useful" of any member of the France family. Every time I see him he is charging out the front door with a baseball glove or a basketball or football in his hand. "Don't go away mad!" his father sometimes calls affably after him, but Eric never acknowledges the joke.

He is slight of build, almost pretty with his long eyelashes and fair complexion, but he is a fierce competitor in sports, and often comes home with cuts and bruises, which Mrs. France is glad to cleanse and bandage because it is almost her only contact with him. I see him tearing along the streets of town on his bicycle more often than I see him at home. Mr. France likes to observe that Eric's metabolism is excessive, which explains both his slenderness and his hyperactivity. I think there is something pent up in Eric that keeps him on the run. I have never figured out what it is, because he rarely deigns to speak to me.

"Tell her I'll be there as soon as Kate finishes with this dress," Lily says.

He doesn't answer. We hear his feet on the stairs and then the bang of the screen door downstairs. We know he has not taken Lily's message.

"Little punk," Lily murmurs. "I could kill him." There is affection in her voice as well as reproach. She likes Eric despite his secrecy and his undependability. They fought angrily when they were younger, perhaps because in their nervous energy they were much alike. Stubborn, excitable, sometimes uncommunicative. But now Lily is the only one besides his mother who seems to know anything about Eric's friends or his doings at school.

Once, when he was a little boy—right in the middle of the fighting period, as a matter of fact—I chanced to pass the door to Lily's room, and saw him lying with his head in her lap, his face covered with tears. She was stroking his hair and murmuring, "Now, now." I never found out what that was about. It would have seemed intrusive to speak to either Lily or Eric about it.

Lily looks at me through the mirror and sighs. "By this time Sunday Jordan will be gone," she says. "What will we do for the rest of our lives, Kate?"

Jordan is leaving for Groton the morning after the ball. This is a pivotal moment for us. We have been a trio all through our childhood, and now we are to be torn apart by the march of time and the claims of the future. At least, we two girls are to be torn from Jordan. I sense behind Lily's excitement about the dress a genuine worry about losing Jordan.

"We'll survive," I say. "And he'll be back for Christmas, anyway. There's nothing to be morbid about."

"Really, Kate. Come with me," she insists. "I'll be nervous on my own."

"I'm not going, and that's final," I say. "But I'll meet you afterward."

It was I who insisted that, as far as the ball itself was concerned, Lily alone was to go as our representative. She and Jordan both protested against this, but I was adamant. I agreed, however, that I would see them later that night.

You may be wondering why such an odd arrangement should have been made by three such close friends, with me as the one insisting on it. A word of explanation is in order.

I was an orphan, my father having died when I was an infant and my mother having later remarried a man who did not wish to be encumbered with a daughter. I was passed from relative to relative until I ended up with an eccentric aunt who lived here in town. When my aunt grew senile enough to need the help of a nurse-companion, there was a hiatus in the availability of relatives able to take me in. Lily's mother, who had always liked me, offered to make room for me in her family. I spent three years with the Frances, until my old aunt died and another set of relatives moved into her house, taking me with them.

I was more of a sister to Lily than her own sisters, because we were identical in age. Though I no longer lived with Lily, I spent at least three or four hours a day with her, doing homework, playing, gossiping, hanging around town—and I had long since given up seeing myself as a lone individual outside our friendship. We breathed as one. At least I had no interest in breathing unless it was part of my relationship with her.

And this is where Jordan comes in.

Lily and I met Jordan at the funeral of a schoolmate who had died of leukemia, a little boy named Peter Gracian. Though Jordan did not go to our school, his mother knew the boy's parents somehow, and brought Jordan to the funeral. Jordan was a very quiet little boy, handsome in an unusual way, with sad eyes and a sweet, winning smile that came out when you encouraged him enough.

Lily and I adopted Jordan on the basis of that first meeting. We did not know at the time that Mrs. France was the only friend Jordan's mother had in the world.

Jordan's mother came from a wealthy and successful local family. Great things had been expected of her, but she made a bad marriage that alienated her from her family and friends before it ended in disaster. When her husband went on a European business trip and disappeared without a trace, he left her with her little son Jordan, then an infant. Lily's mother was the only old friend of Elizabeth's who remained in contact with her.

Jordan fit naturally into the fervid alliance that joined me to Lily. Having lost his father, Jordan understood my orphan status. He was lonely and isolated, and we two girls, however self-sufficient we might have seemed until that time, now felt we needed a third.

I am brutally summarizing something very complicated—in all my later years I have never really understood the early chemistry of that trio, that "threeness" that was to have so important an influence on my whole life. But my lack of clarity corresponds rather well to the friendship itself. We met Jordan, he became part of us without our really knowing why, and the die was cast.

Jordan was the quiet one of the group—shamed by his father's stormy role in the community (of which more later), worried that he would lose us if he made a false move, protective of his exiled mother. I was the ugly duckling, the orphan without a home, eager to feel I belonged somewhere and already fiercely devoted to Lily. As for Lily herself, she completely lacked the chariness about life that affected Jordan and me. She was a free spirit, willful and beholden to no one. Yet she needed us.

She was the leader of our games, the glue that stuck us together, the energy that kept us moving. Throughout our years together Jordan and I always felt we were following in her trail, playing Sancho Panza to her tremendous initiative, her recklessness into which we tapped like famished travelers in a spiritual desert.

But now it has ended. We are to be separated, as Jordan goes off to prep school and we girls stay behind. Adolescence looms over us at the same moment as parting, and so we feel romantic about each other and about our friendship. The ball is to us a deeply symbolic occasion.

But I will not go. I do not want to

be a wallflower, and I don't want to hold Lily back. Though I can't explain myself to Lily, I feel that I cannot experience the true romance of the occasion except by sending her and watching from a distance. I am too ugly, too clumsy to be part of it. Lily is beautiful, and growing more beautiful. I want her to go alone. I am convinced this will not lessen my closeness to Jordan, but will intensify it. The only way I can present myself at that ball, participate in it, is to send her.

After we have finished fitting the dress, Lily wants to take it off, but I insist on showing it to her mother. We go down the stairs from the attic to the bedroom where Mrs. France spends most of her day. She answers our knock with a brisk ''Come in!'' and we enter to find her in bed, as usual, propped up against several pillows.

She doesn't come downstairs much anymore, until dinnertime at least. She was consigned to this routine by her cardiologist, who diagnosed her with congenital heart failure years ago. Once an active and beautiful woman, she is now pale and thin. She is still full of energy, but it seems reined in and distorted by her delicate health. She is in a constant state of frustration about this, and loves to hear us girls tell about our wanderings.

"Look," I said. "Look at Lily!"

Lily pirouettes to show off the dress, and I see in her slim body the image of what her mother used to be. Mrs. France's eyes light up.

"Sweetie, you look wonderful!" she cries. "A real young lady."

Lily comes forward. "Do you think they'll throw me out?" she asks whimsically.

"Perhaps not," Mrs. France replies with her habitual dry humor.

"I can't convince Kate to go," Lily says. "She won't listen to reason. Can't you make her?"

Mrs. France looks at me through eyes that know me very well.

"There's no point in making her do what she doesn't want to do," she says. "It never worked with you, you know that."

And, to me, "But you'll be part of it, won't you, honey?"

"Sure I will."

She knows our plans. We are close enough to her that we do not hide things like this, even things we care deeply about. Something about Mrs. France's semi-invalid status makes her bedroom a refuge to which we can repair, singly or together, for advice and a friendly ear. She seems so much younger than her body, and so able to understand young girls' worries and dreams. To me she has always represented an adult version of Lily, limited by age and illness, but possessed of the same fearless confidence, the same moral agility.

Now her eyes mist a little as she looks at her daughter.

"You're growing up," she says.

"People at Jordan's party will think you're a debutante."

"Oh, Mom." Lily does not like hearing about how fast she is growing.

"It seems like yesterday you were a little hellion rushing in here with skinned knees and a dirty face," Mrs. France says.

There is a pause. Lily stands smiling at her mother in silence.

"All our yesterdays," Mrs. France says.

There is an uncomfortable moment as we let these words sink in. Then she looks at me.

"Honestly," she says. "You two girls look like two peas in a pod sometimes. I think you've spent so much time together that you've got tendrils joining your very bodies."

"Come on!" To me this is absurd. The older Lily grows, the more beautiful she becomes. Every day the process speeds up. While I not only lag behind, a typical slow-maturing teenager, but grow more clumsy every day.

"It's true," says Mrs. France. "You children are too busy putting on makeup to really look at your faces. You don't see what's underneath."

We say nothing to this. She leans back against the pillows, studying the dress.

"Have you shown this to Jordan's mother?" she asks.

"No. We're still getting it to fit."

"Well, I suppose it's best to surprise her," Mrs. France observes uncertainly.

Our high spirits are dampened momentarily by the mention of Jordan's mother. Elizabeth Brady lives in almost complete isolation. Mrs. France talks to her on the phone two or three times a week (graciously ignoring the slurred words which are a result of Mrs. Brady's various tranquilizers and her private drinking) and visits her as often as her faltering health permits. It is an odd situation. The two women have in common their isolation, though in Mrs. France's case it was imposed by illness and in Jordan's mother's case by tragedy. They are intimate friends, and yet Mrs. France always seems briefly worried when we tell her we are on our way to Jordan's house.

"I know Elizabeth will be happy to see you looking so pretty, honey," Mrs. France says. "Be nice to her, now. Times aren't easy for her, you know. With Jordan leaving, especially."

"I'm always nice to her." Lily is a bit impatient with this implied criticism, for even in her wildest years she was nothing but kind to Jordan's troubled, increasingly eccentric mother.

"And she appreciates it," Mrs. France says. "Except for me and Mrs. Dion, you girls and Jordan are her only real contact with the outside world. Now she's going to lose one-third of you. This can't be an easy night for her."

"Oh, Mother," I say, calling her Mother as I sometimes did. "He'll be

back for vacations. He's still just a
boy. She's not losing him.''

"Thirteen is a very important age
for a boy," Mrs. France says, the worried look lingering in her eyes. "Especially when he's going away to
school."

Throughout his childhood Jordan
went to a relatively exclusive private
school about forty miles away, in the
deep woods. It was a school not pa-
tronized by the children of the county
families. Lily and I never reflected on
this, but the fact was that long ago his
parents had selected it for that reason.
Now it was time for him to go on to
Groton, which was part of a plan that
included Yale and Harvard Law.

"He'll be with crowds of boys he's
never met," Mrs. France adds. "No
mother, no father…" At the mention
of Jordan's departed father a slight
flush colors her face. "It won't be the
same," she concludes.

"Well, he'll be the same to his
mother," I insist.

For as long as we have known him, Jordan has been gentle and even courtly toward his mother. As a matter of fact, Lily and I have taken our cue from him in this regard. We always treat the isolated, odd woman with exaggerated courtesy. In return she gives us the run of her enormous house and grounds, and has her servants make us tea or snacks whenever we want them. She seems to consider it a small miracle that we are there for Jordan. She comes out of her fog to greet us, and often to hug us with excessive warmth.

"Oh, my sweet good girls!" she cries. "You look like two perfect flowers in my house. Two sweet little orchids." Her beauty faded by illness and dissolution, she looks at us through sunken eyes and holds out arms stained black and blue by obscure injections.

Often she tries to make conversation with us, but talking to her is difficult. She drags us down tangents that have little to do with the starting point of the conversation, and that do not interest us. Tangents that usually have to do with her own past, her preoccupations. Jordan steps in to extricate us, and as we leave she calls after us in her manic way, "Be good, sweet girls, sweet little girls!" And: "Jordan, be good to your guests!"

Mother sighs, looking at Lily. "I'm glad you're going," she says. "Elizabeth will see you and be reminded that Jordan isn't the only person she has in the world. When he's gone you can go to visit her, as I do. She'll like that." She looks out the window to the distant hills overlooking the ocean, one of which bears the gothic silhouette of the Brady mansion.

This prospect of visiting Mrs. Brady is not altogether pleasing, because she is so difficult to be with. But I can imagine Lily and me going as a duo, armed to protect each other from her strangeness, and getting the latest news of Jordan from her. This will make it all right, I think.

The flush on Mrs. France's cheeks has faded, and she looks pale and suddenly very tired. She is looking at Lily with an expression that makes me suspect she is reminded of her lost youth and health.

"Kiss me," she said.

Lily goes to her side. The thin arms hug her hard.

"Both of you."

I join them, and there is a clumsy moment as both of us lean over the frail woman in the bed. I see that her eyes are dewy again. This makes me a little uneasy for a moment, but then the warm thrill of belonging suffuses me. There is not a hint of jealousy on Lily's part. She is perfectly at ease with the idea that Mrs. France embraces us as though we were twins.

We get up to leave.

"And hug Jordan for me at the dance," Mother calls after us as we close the door.

I insist that we show the dress to Ingrid and Carl before Lily takes it off.

Ingrid, the oldest of the three sisters, is a stay-at-home. She has none of her mother's beauty. She takes after her father's side of the family, as does Carl, the older brother. She is heavy, with dark, sunken eyes and a spinsterish air about her. She is not much fun to be with, but she does have a fierce loyalty to the family, and to her ailing mother.

"Look, Ingrid," I say. "Isn't Lily beautiful?"

I twirl Lily before her. Ingrid comes forward and studies the dress.

"That's good stitching," she says. "That will last." She looks at Lily. "Long after you have any use for it," she adds with a touch of bitterness that is typical of her.

"Oh, Ingrid, cheer up!" Lily laughs. "I'm going to a party."

"Just make sure you don't catch any social diseases over there," Ingrid says.

"Ingrid, you are such a party pooper." Lily frowns, shaking her head.

Ingrid's reference is to the quality of people who come to Mrs. Brady's parties. In the old days, when Mr. Brady was a famous man, most of his guests were successful and well-known people, from the corporate and political worlds, and even from high society. After his disappearance the parties ceased, until, a couple of years ago, Elizabeth took it into her head to revive the tradition. A handful of the old faces reappeared, but most of the guests were little better than hangers-on, representatives of a demimonde on the margins of the business world, and the parties had become a surrealistic ersatz of their old elegance. Mrs. Brady glided through them like a faded pixie, trying valiantly to sprinkle a little of the old opulence, like fairy dust, from her own wand.

Carl is in the upstairs bedroom he has turned into a combined office and workroom. He is a peculiar figure whom I have never really gotten to know. He lives surrounded by electronic equipment, none of which seems to work, and a thousand catalogs and manuals. No one is allowed to clean his room, and it is always full of dust and detritus. His science-fair projects, which won prizes throughout his high school years, remain in the attic, Mrs. France being too nostalgic to throw them away.

He is pleasant enough to adults, but I have always felt that we girls hardly exist for him. As Lily opens the door he looks irritably at us.

"Carl, look at me!" Lily says. "I'm going to Jordan's dance tonight."

Carl pulls his glasses down on his nose and studies Lily. They are like two creatures of different races. Carl is already beginning to lose some of his hair, and, like Ingrid, he is thickening around the middle, which makes him look far older than his years.

"Very nice," he says. "Close the door on your way out."

He glances at me. "Aren't you going to the dance?" he asks.

"No," I say. "I don't like big parties. I wouldn't fit in there."

"Consider yourself fortunate for that," he said.

"Oh, Carl," Lily chides him. "Can't you cheer up?"

"I'm too busy to cheer up. Have a good time."

Lily closes the door on him. "He liked it," she says, indicating the dress. "So did Ingrid. I could tell."

Though I lived for years under the France roof, I am forced to admit that Lily seems to know her siblings far better than I do. Often she shrugs off sarcastic remarks from one or the other of them when I would take offense. At other times she upbraids them severely for things I thought minor. She has a radarlike sensitivity to the significance of all the interactions that take place in the family.

We look for Christine, the youngest girl, in her room. She is not there. The place is a mess. The bed is covered with teen magazines. The little vanity is cluttered with cheap makeup, and pictures of teen idols, rock-and-roll stars and Hollywood heartthrobs are stuck in the border of the mirror.

Christine is already a pretty girl at eleven, but she makes me nervous. She is wild. Not in the natural, tomboyish way that Lily was wild at that age, but in a precocious, driven way that troubles her parents. She hangs out with an unruly crowd at school, and has been the object of numerous parent-teacher conferences from which the Frances returned with tired faces.

"I thought I had worries with Lily," we once overheard Mother telling a friend. "It turns out she was an angel compared to this one. Christine will give me my sleepless nights. She's her father's cross, too."

The Frances are a close family, but the passage of time is fraying the bonds that hold them together. Mr. France is home less often, because the economy is bad for business and he has to spend more time at the store.

Since her mother's illness Lily is the one who does all the little things that keep a family together. She stays around the house a lot. She talks to her siblings and parents. Often she stays in a room to keep other family members from scattering. She intercedes to prevent quarrels between those most likely to be in conflict. Her father seems grateful for this. I often notice him gazing at Lily over his newspaper with a smile of admiration not unlike the one he reserves for his beloved wife.

I am in a position to appreciate this startling change in Lily. When we were little she used to roam far afield and get home late to dinner, incurring her mother's reproaches. A hellion, a tomboy, a wildcat—she was called all these names. But now she seems embedded in her family by her own will, as though to prevent it from splitting apart. I sometimes think she is over-conscientious in this. But as an orphan

I am not equipped to judge such things very well.

I help Lily off with the dress and spend the rest of the afternoon making the final alterations. It is almost as though I am making alterations in myself, alterations that could make me truly perfect for once in my life.

2

Jordan's father was an entrepreneur who came to the county almost by accident on business and met Elizabeth Magnus when he was trying to sell her wealthy father on an idea for some new public transportation companies in Europe.

Mr. Brady was a dashing, handsome fellow with Errol Flynn looks and a brilliant, seductive smile that won people over. He got Mr. Magnus on his side immediately. And for a while, as Mr. Magnus's protégé, he conquered the entire county. Parties were given in his honor, husbands opened their checkbooks to him and—according to rumor—wives fell prey to his almost irresistible charm.

Then he made his mistake. He fell in love with Elizabeth. It turned out that Mr. Magnus's liking for Brady had never included the notion that Brady might try to marry into his society. Despite his polish, Brady clearly came from a less distinguished background. For another thing, he was fifteen years older than Elizabeth and far more experienced. Mr. Magnus vetoed the romance out of hand.

He did not realize that Brady had long since lost the ability to take no for an answer. Brady literally swept Elizabeth off her feet. They eloped together and spent three months in Europe, where he introduced Elizabeth to a style of living appropriate to his own lust for adventure and completely unlike anything she had experienced in her sheltered existence.

They returned, flush with their whirlwind honeymoon and their passion for each other, and discovered to their astonishment that they were both considered *persona non grata* by all the fine families of the county.

Mr. Brady never forgave Elizabeth's friends and relatives for this. He took his pariah status as a challenge. He could have taken Elizabeth away with him to live in

New York or Paris—at the time he certainly could have afforded it—but he did not. Instead he built her an extraordinary house on a hillside overlooking the ocean. He named the place Brookfield, inspiring himself grandly from some obscure memory of Anglo-Saxon aristocracy.

Later he turned a few thousand of the adjoining acres into a championship golf course. He gave lavish parties which were attended by famous people. Society journalists took pictures of him smiling his famous smile alongside senators, congressmen and corporate executives. The county families remained behind their closed doors as the limousines and hired cars serving Brady's gatherings flashed importantly through their midst.

As I say, Brady was a man who would not take no for an answer. He flaunted himself stubbornly before those who ostracized him. He made his house the showplace of their town, and his wife its most famous hostess. But somewhere along the line his stubbornness must have got him in trouble. For he lost all his money, or nearly all of it. He abandoned Elizabeth, who by now was the mother of a little boy. He left enough money at one of his New York banks to provide her with a small annuity, and was heard from no more. Whether he started a new life somewhere else, none of us ever knew. As far as we were concerned, he disappeared into thin air, leaving behind a houseful of photographs of his tanned face and flashing eyes—photographs which would have tormented Elizabeth with their evocation of her disastrous fling, had she not burned them all.

I learned these facts from a combination of accepted local history and rumor, along with occasional reluctant confidences from Mr. and Mrs. France and their older children. These sources formed the store of my childhood knowledge of the Brady family. I suspect they are true, because nothing I saw as a girl at Brookfield contradicts them. On the other hand, one can never know the entire truth about families. Even the best family has obscure corners that are resistant to truth, either because they are kept secret or because they are enigmas for which there is no simple answer. I was to realize this as I grew up, not only about other people but about myself.

In any case, only the Brady house remained, its countless rooms mostly closed up now that Elizabeth had withdrawn into a tiny corner of the mansion near the main kitchen. The windows glowed golden at sunset as though remembering the brilliant evenings that once enlivened the place. The spacious lawns and gardens, jungle-like since all the gardeners had been fired, made the perfect setting for our games of hide-and-seek, while Jordan's mother remained inside with her medicines and her spirits and her memories. Mrs. Dion, the loyal housekeeper, was her only companion other than Jordan. No car came up the mile-long driveway except that of Elizabeth's attorney. And, once in a while, the old station wagon driven by Lily's mother.

On our last night the ball starts early, for Jordan is to leave first thing tomorrow morning. A bizarre assortment of guests assembles, most of whom barely know who Jordan is. But Elizabeth, circulating nervously among them, manages through a climactic effort of will to create an atmosphere of gaiety and collective congratulation. The lawns have been mowed, the shrubs trimmed, and colored lights hang from the trees, casting a glow which seems to turn back the clock on all the empty years, as couples dance to the music of a ten-piece orchestra.

I am watching from behind one of the hedges. I stayed at home as the Brady car came to collect Lily. A corsage was brought for me as well, but I left it in its box in my bedroom. I walked here through the balmy night and lurked on the outskirts of the party until I saw Jordan and Lily.

They are on the dance floor now. Other couples have turned to look at them. Elizabeth, haggard and magnificent, has paused in her circulation to beam her smile upon them.

They both look a little nervous, and for a moment I feel a pang of worry that my efforts as a seamstress have been inadequate. But now I see people coming up to meet Lily, to shake hands with her, and I see them compliment her on her dress. She blushes, and the color in her cheeks makes her seem even more unreal, even more like a princess.

I am too young to perceive the decay and humiliation about which Carl and Ingrid warned Lily and me. In my eyes the occasion is grave and magnificent, the guests are talking about beautiful adult things. That many of them are drunk I will realize only in memory, many years from now.

Jordan is wearing a white tie and tails that make him look very much the important young man about to leave home and accomplish great things. His face is tanned, and his dark eyes, with their tinge of sadness, make a marvelous contrast with the expectant smile on his face. He scans the crowd as though looking for me, but Lily says something in his ear and he nods acknowledgment.

They both look different tonight, as though time has speeded up around them. The old Lily, the younger one, would have been gazing around unselfconsciously at the guests, and perhaps giggling at those whose appearance amused her. But tonight she looks demure and even diffident, standing a bit in Jordan's shadow as though afraid to be seen.

Then they begin to dance. Jordan dances beautifully, holding Lily with tender grace as he twirls her around the floor. Every time she turns in my direction I see her eyes look for me; she knows approximately where I planned to station myself.

The older couples join in as though taking their cue from Jordan and Lily. A slight coolness has stolen into the air, increasing the energy of the moment. I stand in the shadows, watching. My cheeks are moist, but I notice no tears coming from my eyes. I am bewitched by my certainty that, on this night, the whole world is pausing to admire Lily, and to bind her to Jordan.

Something is changing in me at this moment, as I watch my two best friends whirl about that dance floor. I am only half there in the shadows. The other half of me is out on the dance floor, wrapped around Lily and Jordan like a ghost. It is as though I am willingly relinquishing a hold on myself as a separate person that I may never regain. I sense the fatefulness of this change. I even suspect that, in the future, as a grown woman, I may regret it. But I don't care. I am living dangerously as I watch my two friends. I am drunk with my own indifference to the consequences.

A voice startles me.

"I'm afraid you can't be here, miss."

I turn to see a man I recognize as one of Jordan's mother's servants, dressed in an unfamiliar livery which vaguely suggests he is acting as a security guard.

"Oh, I'm sorry," I say. "I was just watching Jordan and Lily."

The servant glances over the hedge.

"I didn't recognize you in this darkness, Miss Kate. Why aren't you at the ball yourself?"

He is Stanford, one of the servants who were here in Brady Sr.'s time. He is very proper in his manner, very respectful. As the corps of servants has grown smaller and smaller, he has taken on the role of representing the old guard. He does it with deliberate courtliness. He is very devoted to Elizabeth.

I ponder for a moment. I don't want to tell him the truth, but I don't want him to throw me out, either.

"Weren't you invited, miss?" he asks.

"Oh, I was," I say. "But I wasn't feeling too well tonight, so I decided to stay home. But I just wanted to see Lily in her dress."

"Well, that's fine," he says. "But you shouldn't be standing out here alone in the dark. You'll catch cold."

He looks at the dancers.

"They do make a lovely couple, miss," he observes.

"Yes, they do," I agree.

"Just perfect for each other," he says.

I am impressed to hear an outsider put my own thoughts into words. Lily and Jordan look so perfect together, so ideally matched, with her bright agility and Jordan's sad dark eyes. Caught at this moment of their rapid growth, they are the same height and size, and it occurs to me that they look like twins. Not siblings, though—twins in a different, deeper sense. As though they shared a particular essence which joins them in their very flesh, though they are so different in spirit.

"You should be out there, too, miss," Stanford says. "You would look pretty, yourself, dancing with Master Jordan."

I say nothing. How can I explain to him that my place is out here in the darkness, that in this place I feel more excited and fulfilled than I ever could on that dance floor? It would be almost like admitting a crime to usurp Lily's rightful place in the spotlight.

His eyes scan the guests.

"Well, it's not like the old days, miss," he says. "When Mr. Brady was here, the ball was a great event."

I don't reply. The orchestra has started a waltz, and Jordan and Lily have started off in a circular motion. I think I see her blush at something he says.

"Yes, times change," Stanford says. "Nothing stays what it was. But that's the way of the world." He looks at me. "Soon we old folks will be out of the way, and it will be up to you young people to make the world all over again."

I knew Stanford was of a thoughtful turn of mind, and a depressive one. I don't pay much attention to his words.

But at that moment, vaguely aware as I am that the ball is no longer the grand affair it was when Mr. Brady lent it all his arrogance and energy, I do feel that a new world will one day replace this dying one, and that Jordan and Lily, whirling under those lights to that sweet, wistful music, are the people who will build it. My faith in them, and in myself through them, is boundless. Surely the magic of tonight is more than capable of a little thing like changing the world.

"Maybe you're right," I say, turning to Stanford. But he has disappeared. Perhaps he got tired of waiting for me to answer. I don't know how long I was lost in thought.

I'm glad I am alone again. Now I can give myself completely to my contemplation of Jordan and Lily. It is not a thing I wish to share with anyone else. It belongs to me alone.

Late that night the three of us meet on the golf course that occupies several hundred of the vast acres surrounding the house. The course is overgrown, the fairways looking like pastures, the greens like little glades set incongruously among the tall trees. But it was designed by one of the finest golf course architects in the world. Jordan's father had it built in order to shame the course of the local country club that would not admit him as a member.

Many of the holes were designed for the vistas they offered, as well as for the challenge they presented. There were several high spots with views of the distant ocean, and others which offered views of the house, sparkling with gothic grandeur in the morning light or turning a golden purple as the sun set.

In those days the course was kept in perfect condition, the cups placed in championship positions. It was written up by all the best golf magazines, and some of the top professionals played it as Brady's guests. Ben Hogan himself was quoted as saying that Brady's thirteenth hole was "the best par four I have ever played in my life."

But nearly all the time Brady played the course alone. When he was not out of town on business, he could be seen in his plus-fours, accompanied by his caddy, ostentatiously playing his beautiful holes with clubs made for him in Scotland. Despite his pleas, Elizabeth would not play with him. She did not like golf, she said. He suspected she did not want to expose herself by going out of the house.

The golf course, like the parties, was Brady's way of thumbing his nose at his county neighbors. He wanted them to feel the inferiority of their hidebound life to his adventurous one. He knew they talked about him behind his back; he wanted to make sure there was envy mingled with their disapproval.

After Brady's disappearance, the decay that was overtaking Brookfield seemed to begin with the golf course, Brady's prized possession. Elizabeth fired the mowers and maintenance people. The fairways became overgrown. The flags were tattered, billowing haggardly in the cups that were full of dirty rainwater. The sand traps had permanent puddles. The oaks and willows, which had once been carefully trimmed by workmen to create just the right hazard, were shaggy now, and when autumn came they dropped their leaves in great piles that were never cleaned up.

The overgrown golf course was the visible symbol of Elizabeth's abandonment and of the destruction of Brady's dreams. And it was here, among the hirsute fairways, the forgotten tees and empty greens, that our childhood trio found its greatest intimacy.

We wandered the course in the afternoons. I can still remember it in the spring, when long, dewy grass moistened our legs, when cattails grew where they shouldn't have and dandelions attacked the turf. And in the summer, when the sun burned the untended grass brown. And most of all in the fall, when the dying leaves made a riot of color, the sun warming our faces while the brisk breezes of October whipped our cheeks to a red flush.

The famous thirteenth hole, admired by Ben Hogan in his memoirs, had a name, as did all the other holes, in the British tradition. It was called the Fertile Crescent. This sobriquet referred not only to its shape—a sharp dogleg which forced the player to shoot blind around a thicket of tall pines—but to the fact that the new moon was visible from the tee as it rose over the ocean several days each month. It was a lofty, extraordinary view, and it grew more dramatic as the sun dropped lower in the sky. From this vantage point you couldn't tell how near or far the ocean really was. It depended on the light, the sky, the water, and even your mood. Sometimes it seemed distant as the next county. At other times, especially when it was warm, you could look down from that elevated spot and almost feel the water cooling your toes.

If distance was an enigma up here, so was time. As you looked from the eternal waves to the gothic stateliness of the house, the twentieth century was nowhere in view. You felt you were being enfolded in a mythic past that protected you from all the accidents the future might bring.

The slope of the hill from the tee was so sharp that we children used it for sledding in the winter. In the warmer seasons we had picnics on the tee, and played hide-and-seek among the huge trees ringing the hitting area.

I used to stand on that thick grass, with Jordan and Lily somewhere nearby, and feel as though my earlier self from previous visits was calling to me in the rustle of the trees. And the self I had not yet glimpsed, but would one day become, seemed only a whisper away, telling me secrets about my fate in a language I almost understood, but not quite.

I don't know whether Jordan and Lily felt as I did, but I do know we tended to fall into elegiac moods whenever we were up there. One year we visited the place almost every day. Then we began to save it for special times. We would play our usual games elsewhere, but when a wind-whipped afternoon, a lowering sky or a soft summer rain told us a special mood was coming, we would go up to the Fertile Crescent.

So it is natural that tonight, for our goodbye on the eve of Jordan's departure, we decide to come here.

I am waiting in the darkness when they come from the house, two glowing figures gliding through the trees, their smiles lit by the hovering moon.

"Oh, Kate!" Lily throws her arms around me. "It was so wonderful. Did you see?"

Jordan hugs me, too. Then he takes both my hands and holds me out so he can look at me.

"You should have been with us," he says.

"Oh, I didn't want to. I liked it better from where I was."

He holds me a moment longer. He seems disturbed by my queer preference for solitude. Then, on an impulse, he pulls me closer and begins to dance with me. Lily hums in encouragement as he whirls me around in the grass. I feel the sudden, sweet incidence of his flesh and his youth, and now the tears I had fought back earlier come forward too suddenly for me to stop them.

"What's the matter?" Jordan asks, still holding me.

"Nothing," I say. "You're just so handsome. And Lily is so pretty. Everything is so perfect. Just like we hoped."

"And you?" he asks.

I don't answer. We dance until I am tired, and then we wander down the fairway toward the ocean. Jordan and Lily are still in their formal clothes, and, like all young actors in a very important play, will not take them off until morning.

"Let's make this night last forever," Lily says.

We stay up all night, talking about the party, the guests, Jordan's plans for Groton, our own plans for the year to come. We talk about our past. We hold hands. At times, as though for no reason, I see tears in my friends' eyes, or feel the scene distorted by my own welling tears.

When a gray glow in the east tells us morning is coming, we sense a new urgency in our last hour together.

Lily suddenly sits forward. "I've got an idea," she says. "Let's meet right here in this spot someday. A long time from now."

Tired but interested, we both look up at her.

"You're right," I say. "We can't let ourselves be separated, just because we have to grow up."

Her legs are crossed under her dress, which flows out around her, making her look like a pale pink flower in the moonlight. She is leaning back, and her slender arms look particularly delicate and graceful. Jordan is watching her.

"How long shall we wait?" he asks.

"Ten years," I say.

There is a silence. Fatigue is overcoming all three of us, but instead of attenuating our concentration on this sudden plan, it intensifies it.

"No," Lily says. "That's not long enough. We'll only be twenty-three in ten years."

"Twenty years, then."

"No," Jordan puts in. "By then we'll be thirty-three."

"I don't ever want to be thirty-three!" Lily cries.

I have to laugh at this, though I don't know why. Lily looks so determined that it does indeed seem she might somehow find a way to never be thirty-three.

Jordan is gazing at her with a quiet

fascination that tells me he is thinking something similar.

"Fifteen years, then." I don't notice which of us says this, but it brings immediate agreement.

"We'll be twenty-eight. Twenty-eight is a perfect age," says Lily.

"Old enough to know what you're doing," I say.

"Old enough to be taken seriously," says Lily.

"Old enough to really remember," adds Jordan.

"What do you mean?" I ask.

"I'm not sure," Jordan replies. "I just think you need to have lived before you can really remember something important. I don't want to remember this moment just next week, or next year. In fifteen years I'll know how to appreciate it."

Lily is looking at him through eyes dark with empathy.

"You're right, Jordan," she says. "We're too young now." And she takes his hand.

I agree with her choice of words. Our promise, like Lily's elegant dress and Jordan's formal suit, is serious beyond our years. We dare to commit ourselves this way because we trust the future to do what our hearts desire. Our love makes us bold.

"What if we forget?" I ask.

"We won't forget," Jordan replies. "If you want something badly enough, it will come true."

He draws me to him, and the three of us are embracing.

"Fifteen years," Lily repeats.

"Right here on this hill."

We look around us at the place that has been the scene of so many of our most exalted moments. The moon is sinking toward the horizon like an omen compelling us to this pact.

"Then we'll be together forever," I say. "That will be the proof."

As we watch, the ocean begins to change color. In an instant, it seems, the sky is beginning to brighten toward day. We feel as though a spell is being broken. We hurry back toward the house, following a well-known route along the brick paths between the fairways. I seem to see us from far behind, a disembodied eye watching wistfully as the trio to which I belong recedes into future time, eternally young.

That's where my memory ends. I don't know how Lily and I got home, or how late we slept, or whether we talked about what had happened. I don't remember whether we went to the station to see Jordan off. I don't remember a thing.

Except this. A few days after Jordan's departure, Elizabeth Brady committed suicide. In a small, rarely used bathroom deep in an abandoned wing of the great house, she slashed her wrists and waited in a full bathtub for her life to drain out of her.

Her suicide note was addressed to her son. No one ever found out what it said.

3

Many years have passed since that bewitched moment on an overgrown golf course, a place that once represented the willful arrogance of Brady's father, then the vengeful negligence of his abandoned wife, and finally, for one moonlit night, the dreams of three adolescents gathered into a single dream.

Not all those described above are even alive now. The date of the promised rendezvous is long past. Its passage, and its effects, are themselves part of history.

As I think these thoughts, the sounds of birds reach my ears, the voices of children, the barking of a dog. Reassuring sounds which remind me of those years with Lily, though I now live in a time and place far removed from our past together. The room around me, decorated only a couple of years ago, is already familiar, taking on the patina of habit, a warm refuge for my middle years. A room away there is someone who knows I am here, someone who anticipates my step, my voice. I am not alone. I will not be alone.

My life has "worked itself out," as we say. I have developed, I have changed. I'm not the same person I was when I lay in the arms of my two friends on that moonlit, overgrown fairway and dreamed of a future that—of course—has not come to pass as we imagined it.

Who remembers a rendezvous promised at age thirteen? What adult person even remembers himself at thirteen? Time moves forward, never backward. The things we felt so deeply at that "transitional" age were confused to begin with and thus all the more easy to outgrow, to forget. If we didn't forget them we would never grow up. That is common wisdom. I can hardly refute it.

Yet something tells me it is wrong, the life we live. We let the best of ourselves slip through our fingers, and we don't even think to bid it farewell. When old people have lost touch with present time and only retain their earliest memories, they are called senile. That may be true, but I think all of us are senile in another way. We are so busy worrying about tomorrow, and the events leading most directly to tomorrow, that we never bother to view the larger ocean of time among whose slow currents we have struggled to find ourselves. Nor do we wonder about the ripples left by our very struggles, and their unexpected effects on the future.

We are only aware of the nearest moments of time. We have forgotten the most important ones.

When Lily and I were small girls she fell off the roof of my aunt's house one night. We had sneaked out there after dark in hopes of catching a glimpse of the Carmichael girl next door with her boyfriend. They were in the habit of necking in an upstairs room of her house. It was Lily who had discovered this and dragooned me into joining her in this expedition. More preco-

cious than I, she was fascinated by the doings of teenage girls.

We waited until my aunt was asleep and
climbed out onto the roof through a dormer
window in the unused upstairs bedroom.
The roof was steeper than I had anticipated,
and I wanted to go back. But Lily wouldn't
hear of it. "Stop being a sissy!" she hissed
in my ear. "Come on!"

We crawled clumsily along the roof in
our bare feet. I think we did catch a brief
glimpse of two adolescent faces locked in a
lingering kiss. I looked at Lily, who was
crouching on the harsh tar paper shingles,
her eyes locked to the target. I noticed that
she had scraped her knee. Her blood shone
as a dark gleam in the moonlight. She
seemed not to have noticed the injury.

I must have been lost in thought for a
moment or two as I felt the chill night air
on my skin and glanced up at the hovering
moon. I heard a noise. I turned to see Lily
sliding precipitously down the roof. She had
lost her footing. As I watched in horror, she
disappeared.

I climbed down to the gutter, feeling the

shingles score the palms of my hands, and found her hanging there, looking up at me with a panic in her eyes that I had never seen before.

"Pull me up," she said. "Pull me up, Kate!"

I took hold of her wrist. But before I could get enough balance to steady myself on the sloping roof, the old gutter came loose with a screech and Lily fell all the way to the grass at the side of the house. Had she landed on the driveway she might have broken both legs or even killed herself; as it was, she suffered a bad ankle fracture and was in a cast for six weeks.

I'm sure we were punished by my aunt for our misdemeanor, though I have no memory of that. Lily recovered the full use of her ankle, but her walk was never quite the same again. We rarely talked about the episode.

Once in a while, as I drift in and out of dreams at night, I see Lily's terrified face receding from me, farther and farther, as gravity and our own childish foolishness pulled her down to the hard unforgiving earth. And as I float toward waking consciousness, I remember the day I dared to observe, some time after Lily had healed, that her walk was a little different. She denied it hotly. "It's the same as it always was," she said. I never mentioned it again.

Only in the world of dreams, where forbidden things are allowed, does the image of Lily's fall come forward and show itself to me. By morning it is forgotten. Yet Lily's recklessness, and later her fierce refusal to concede anything to life, including her own broken bones, are real parts of me, as real as the face I see in the mirror every morning.

Perhaps I don't think about them because they reflect other parts of me which I am not very proud of. Lily's daring reminds me of my own cautiousness about myself and other people—a cautiousness that has sometimes held life at arm's length when I should have been embracing it, taking chances for it. This is, I am afraid, another price of being an orphan. One never expects the world to be kind. One is constantly taking inner precautions against a disaster that might be around the next corner.

For a long time I didn't think about such things. I was too busy with my current interests and plans. I moved ahead with life, a purposeful adult, and didn't look back. I gained something, to be sure, by refusing to listen to my past. But I also lost something of myself, a thing that called out and was never heeded because my grown-up ears were not attuned to it. I saw my face in the mirror, but not the reality behind it. As Mrs. France cannily observed of us girls, I was too busy applying makeup to see the real person underneath the face I was putting on.

But a cork floating atop an ocean can only make believe it is independent for so long. Sooner or later the whispering depth that supports it must be heard. I could not put it off forever.

4

Times had changed. The recession had hurt the economy badly; the economic downturn that followed destroyed our whole nation's sense of its own security. No one, it turned out, was safe from this quicksand that took the ground out from under our feet.

The county families found, to their astonishment, that their old money was no match for the crisis. They had to sell out and move away to less costly places. Within a few years most of the houses along the ocean had been sold to new owners. It was a real-estate bonanza, the stately old places being bought up by people who were making their money in advertising or computers or soft drinks. Flashier people with new money, who lived in a new way.

Throughout the country there was a stunning change of mood about life. People were hunkered down, teeth clenched, waiting to endure the next blow that might come. The old sense of expectation, of idealism, had died as quickly as it had flared into life. It was not easy to be happy anymore. Nor was it pleasant to think about the future.

I had left Summer Harbor to go to high school in Oregon, where my closest relatives lived. I was too far away to come back and visit the Frances. In those days the long-distance phone bills seemed high, so my relationship with Lily was reduced to letter-writing.

My own letters would embarrass me terribly if I saw them today. They were filled with cloying idealizations of our friendship and confused yearnings about the future. I gradually got the feeling that Lily was impatient with my woolgathering. Her own letters grew more matter-of-fact. Her old humor was there, and she did make occasional reference to our old private jokes and rituals. ''Pink Fingers'' and ''Bottomless Pit,'' the nicknames that referred respectively to her addiction to pistachio nuts and my appetite for her mother's cooking, were mentioned. But the exultation we had once shared was quickly ebbing away. Hers were the letters of a girl on a fast road to adulthood. Mine were those of someone who was having a hard time making up her mind to leave the illusions of youth behind.

It was not until the spring of my senior year that I was able to manage a trip to Summer Harbor. I quickly saw that there were more reasons than time itself for the change in Lily. Her family had lost all its money. Her father's business, never very healthy to begin with, had collapsed in the recession. A man in his sixties now, Mr. France could not find work and had no choice but to retire.

The disaster had affected the entire family. Lily's brother Carl had dropped out of college and gone to work selling advertising space for the local newspaper. He had had little choice in the matter; but I sensed relief in his withdrawal from ambition. He was a quiet, retiring man, cut from his father's cloth, and it was clear he had never been comfortable with the burden of worldly accomplishment.

As for Mr. France himself, he still seemed mild and smiling, but much older now. Most of the time he sat in a chair in the living room, or in his office out back, staring out the window. When Lily brought me to meet him he seemed to have some difficulty recognizing me. Since I had lived for three years under his roof, this strongly suggested he was not the man he had been.

''What's Ingrid up to these days?'' I asked Lily.

''She's just finishing nurses' college,'' Lily replied. ''She says there's always work for an RN. I think it will be perfect for her.''

I was to learn that Ingrid was spending most of her time with Mrs. France, whose health had continued to deteriorate. I suspected that she had an ulterior motive for training as a nurse. She intended to help her mother through what promised to be a long illness, and in so doing to save the family the prohibitive cost of round-the-clock nursing.

"What about the younger generation?" I asked, using the family's nickname for Eric and Christine.

"Useless as ever, both of them," Lily said. "Eric comes home a couple of times a week, it seems. The rest of the time he's out with those scummy friends of his, doing whatever it is they do. Christine runs with an even worse crowd, but at least she comes home for dinner."

Lily seemed genuinely hurt by this disloyalty of the younger siblings. I failed to understand what it was that had alienated them so dramatically from their parents. Lily's mother turned pale every time Eric's name was mentioned, and Mr. France only came out of his fog when he cross-examined Christine about her friends and whereabouts. There were arguments in which Christine angrily assured him she was up to nothing. But a single glance at her pretty, rebellious face—covered with far too much makeup—left no doubt that she was into some sort of mischief when away from home. I was there long enough to see some of the boys who came to pick her up, and I could understand the parents' worry.

The family was crystallizing, but not in a happy way. The older siblings were settling into the role of stay-at-homes while the younger ones rebelled.

And Lily was right in the middle.

She had done very well in high school, earning good grades and distinguishing herself in numerous extracurricular activities, including track and field. She had grown even more attractive and had a lot of dates. In her letters she had told me she was planning to go to the state university at Orono and perhaps on to graduate school. She hoped to get scholarships based on her grades and her family's financial woes. Mr. and Mrs. France, both college graduates, were astonished and chagrined to reflect that Lily might be the only one of their five children to finish college.

As soon as I saw Lily, I understood the change in her letters. The world we once took for granted had fallen apart around her, and she was girding herself to survive. This burden had changed her physically as well as emotionally. She looked older, less impulsive.

"You don't look like your pictures," I said.

"What do you mean?"

"You're prettier, for one thing," I hazarded tactfully. "But you look so much—smoother."

"Smoother!" She laughed, wrinkling her freckled nose. "That's a funny thing to say about a person." I thought I heard a note of defensiveness behind this.

"Like a woman," I said quietly. "More—more polished."

"Did you know we're probably going to move next spring?" she said.

This announcement shocked me, coming *apropos* of nothing. I looked around at the house I had thought about so often during my long exile from it, and tried without success to imagine the Frances without it.

"Why?" I asked.

"It's too fancy an address," she said. "The mortgage is too much. Daddy thinks we have to move. Besides, we're all growing up. So we don't need all this space."

There was a brittle tone in her voice, and I knew she regretted the loss of the place.

"Where will you move?" I asked.

"They're building some new subdivisions over toward Reedsburg," she said. "Cute little places, actually. I can drive you over and show you while you're here."

I looked at the house. "I'll miss it," I said. "Some of my happiest memories are here. Remember the night we made the sauerkraut, and the pressure cooker blew up?"

She smiled ruefully, embarrassed by her own memory. In her smile was none of the old wildness that had once been part and parcel of her, but something else which seemed familiar though I could not identify it.

"Oh, yes," she said. "Those good old days."

"And the time I got my tongue stuck on the freezer wall?" I pursued. "I thought I was going to die."

Again Lily smiled. And this time I recognized the smile. It was her mother's smile. The smile of a woman who has become tolerant of life, who accepts it grace-

fully despite its heartaches. Suddenly I
missed the old Lily. I realized my nostalgic
comments had been intended to draw her
out, and had failed. Lily was a grown-up
now. Life had taken from her the luxury of
being a girl. Since I myself did not feel
grown-up, this made me feel lonely.

"So how are the men treating you?" she
asked suddenly.

I had to think this over quickly. I was
eighteen years old and I had never had a
man friend.

"Not bad, not good," I lied. "You know
how men are. I'm sure it will be better in
college." I had applied to NYU for journalism, and Lily knew it.

"The big city," she mused. "It will be
good for you. You've been in too small a
pond."

"Let's just hope that *I'm* not too small a
pond," I said. "New York scares me a little."

"Nonsense," she said. "You'll do fine.
This is what you've been waiting for." It
was an odd choice of words, but I thought
she was perhaps right. I had been waiting

for something, ever since I left Lily. And so far it had not come.

"Come on," she said. "Let's take a walk."

We left my stuff in her room and went down the old staircase to the front. Everything seemed eloquently the same—the threadbare rug on the stairs, the banister with its smell of lemon polish, the old couches in the living room. I hated the thought of losing that house. But there wasn't time to linger over that now.

We walked down Hibbard Avenue to Third Street and took the "back way" toward town. I recognized all the old houses, though they were sporting new cars, small children's bicycles and basketball hoops that had not been there before. It was still the same town, but time had it in its grip, and the people inside these houses were strangers.

"Shall I tell you about my fella?" Lily asked.

"Absolutely." She had mentioned him in her letters, but not gone into any detail.

"Well, he's in his third year at North-

western,'' she said. ''He wants to be a law-
yer, even though his father wants him to
take over the family business when he graduates.'' She looked at me. ''You remember
the Sewells, don't you? Over on Parkridge
Crest?''

''The Sewells? Sure.'' I vaguely remembered a family whose sons and daughters
went through our school with relentless distinction. There was always a Sewell on the
debating team or the baseball team or the
cheerleading squad. I had the impression
they came from old money. The girls were
all debutantes, and the boys were headed
for Ivy League schools.

''Well, this is Rob. He graduated before
you left.''

I looked at Lily in surprise. Rob Sewell
was not the boy she had been mentioning
in her letters.

''But...I thought you were going steady
with that other boy,'' I said. ''Randy...''

She looked impatient.

''No. Rob's the one. We're getting married in June.''

I was stunned, the more so because Lily had told me the news in so casual a way.

"Really," I said.

"His father doesn't want him to marry me," she said. "At least until he graduates and decides about his future. But Rob doesn't care what his father thinks. He wants to start a family right away."

I listened, hiding my amazement, as she filled in the details. The Sewells had lost money in the recession, like everybody else. But Mr. Sewell, smarter than his neighbors and more energetic, had amassed a second fortune in the construction business over the past decade and a half. It was his firm that had built most of the newer commercial buildings in town, and had contracts with the county and state for schools and other public buildings. The Sewells were the only "old money" family left in the county that was still prosperous.

Rob's conflict with his father came from the problem of the business. Mr. Sewell was a rough-hewn, picky man who didn't trust his subordinates. He rightly felt that he had saved his family from ruin by the sweat of his own brow, and he wanted Rob, his most talented son, to see that the business remained prosperous. But Rob disdained the crude day-in-day-out grind of business, and wanted his own life.

That's where Lily came in. Rob had been patiently carrying a torch for her ever since a casual date two years before. He took her swimming before an evening at the movies, and the sight of her slender body moving along the beach at Chandlers Cove, a few grains of sand clinging to her tanned calves as she breathed in the air of dusk, had haunted him ever since.

He confided this to me much later, along with the fact that he knew he was just one of a dozen beaux. He was not blind to the fact that in Lily there was something unusual, something light-years removed from the charms of ordinary girls. It might be impossible to win her, and even if he succeeded there might be a larger impossibility of ever really possessing her. But he did not give up. And that spring, suddenly, without warning, she had accepted him.

The father and son were very different

men. Mr. Sewell was stocky and florid, and often smoked a cigar which he chomped furiously between his ruddy jaws. He had the look of an entrepreneur about him, and contrasted with the county gentry so much that in the old days many of them had not liked to socialize with him despite his illustrious family background.

Rob was taller, slimmer, and had inherited his mother's good looks, with dark hair and soft, reflective eyes. He was politically liberal, which created a climate of constant argument with his dyed-in-the-wool Republican father.

The two men played golf together, and Mr. Sewell, competitive by nature, watched in consternation as Rob learned to beat him at an early age. Mr. Sewell was an aggressive player, swatting at the ball with strokes so violent that they sometimes hurt his back. Rob had an easy swing, and an approach to the game so relaxed that it was a wonder he could break eighty nearly every time out. It looked as though he wasn't even trying.

Mr. Sewell was not happy about Rob's

decision to shun the family business in favor of law school. But he elected not to force the issue, for he was subtle enough to see that an outright war might make him lose his son.

"Why doesn't he want him to marry you?" I asked Lily. "Doesn't Mr. Sewell like you?"

"Oh, he likes me all right," she said. "He even pinches my cheek and calls me honey. But he wants somebody better for Rob."

"Who could be better than you?" I asked.

"Lots of girls," Lily said. "I'm not much, you know. Socially, anyway."

I could not deny the logic of this. The Sewells were the only county family that had survived the economic crisis with real wealth and future prospects intact. It would have made sense for Rob to marry a girl from a fine old family. But he had made up his mind that he wanted Lily.

"He's eager to meet you," Lily said. "He wants you to come along on our date tonight."

"Oh, I couldn't," I said.

"You've got to! He'll be disappointed!" Lily said with unexpected vehemence.

Then she calmed down. "Besides, I want to show him off." Suddenly she put her arm through mine. "And to show you off."

We were coming to the junction of Route 12, where, in the distance, Brookfield suddenly came into view, looking remarkably pretty in the gilded light of afternoon.

"It's still there," I said.

"Oh, yes, it's still there," Lily said. "Somebody keeps paying the taxes on it, or the mortgage, or whatever. Some of the newer people in town have complained about it because it's such a wreck. But there's nothing they can do."

"You'd never know to look at it," I said.

"Oh, it's a ruin," Lily said. "No one goes over there but mischievous children and teenagers for petting parties. One of them fell into the swimming pool a couple of years ago and broke a leg or something."

From a distance the house was strikingly intact. Its slate roof and leaded windows gave it a look of dignified permanence that effectively masked the decay one might have seen from a closer vantage point.

"I wonder what the golf course looks like now," I said.

Lily didn't answer.

"Have you heard from Jordan?" I asked, watching the easy swing of Lily's purse as she walked beside me. The waning sun seemed to caress her eyes with flecks of gold that shone in the deep blue irises.

"He went to college overseas, I think." There was something evasive in her tone.

For a brief second I wondered whether Lily's association with Jordan Brady, and her mother's well-known association with Elizabeth, might have anything to do with the resistance of a family like the Sewells. Then I decided that was all ancient history. No one could remember those old days. They were another world.

Lily had taken my arm again to turn me back toward home.

"You're going to like him," she said. "You'll see."

"Who?" I asked.

"Rob, silly."

I did like him. He was a handsome boy, gentle-looking despite his considerable height—he was six-three at least—and a strong, attractive build. He had a deep tan, probably from his golfing outings, and very white teeth which showed handsomely when he smiled. And he smiled often, mostly at Lily.

"Do you play golf, Kate?" he asked me.

"No, I don't," I said. "I once visited a driving range, but the results were disastrous."

"I'm trying to get Lily to play golf with me," he said. "She's got natural ability, but she won't learn. She keeps saying it's too social at the country club."

We had gone to the movies and were on our way to a local restaurant. At that particular moment Lily was walking ahead of us. The sidewalk glistened under her firm strides.

Rob slowed his pace until she was far enough ahead not to overhear him. "I love the way she walks," he murmured to me. "I never thought I could fall in love with the way a woman walked."

Surprised by this sudden confidence from a young man who had been rather reserved all evening, I glanced at his face. The look in his eyes was almost stricken. *Lovesick,* I thought. The word described him perfectly.

Over our dinner we argued about women's liberation and joked about the people we knew in common. Rob rarely took his eyes off Lily. As for me, I tried to see her through his eyes. She had changed. There was something settled and almost languid about her. She stated opinions and made observations in a careless, relaxed way that suggested nothing meant so terribly much to her in the world outside her own family circle. Except us two, of course. Her smile seemed to gather us in and warm us.

There was a touching affection between her and Rob, though they were not demonstrative about it either at the movies or afterward. He would hold her hand for a few seconds while we talked, put his arm on her shoulder or at the small of her back. He seemed aware that she was too independent a girl for him to hover over. Yet, in the space he gave her, she nestled somehow, reminding him through small signs that she was his.

It was a pleasant evening, but it left me feeling perplexed. Lily and I stayed up late, gossiping and talking about the wedding, and I gave her plenty of opportunities to open up more about Rob. But she didn't. When I went to my old room to sleep, I felt memories of our years together gathering around me in the shadows. The old house was like a friend, all the more precious for the fact that it was soon to be taken out of our lives.

I felt as though I had come home. But at the same time I felt as though Lily had left it before I got there. Everything was slipping away, not only because of the world outside but because of Lily herself.

Lily and Rob were married that June. I came down to be her maid of honor. The night before the wedding she helped me try on my dress.

It was too long, and as Lily was hemming it, I could not help remembering the night

long ago when it had been me fixing her
dress, not here in her bedroom but upstairs
in the attic, with Jordan Brady's ball her
destination.

When the dress was finished she took me
in to show it to her mother. Mrs. France was
much weaker now, and was going to have
to be taken to and from the wedding in a
wheelchair. But she had welcomed me as
warmly as ever, and her old spirit was un-
dimmed.

"Sweetie, you look like a picture," she
said.

"Thanks, Mom." I used the old endear-
ment deliberately, enjoying the sound of it
on my lips. Mrs. France was the only
mother I had ever known. Though she had
five children of her own, those wonderful
eyes had always rested on me with the bottomless approval and delight of a mother.
During the past few years I had written her
almost as often as I had written Lily. I could
not look at her wasted body without thinking about how much I would miss her when
she was gone.

"Lily, turn her around," she said. As

Lily twirled me, her mother sat up to study the lines of the dress.

"You know, Kate, you're quite the young lady yourself," she said. "I hope they're ready for you in New York."

"Thanks." I blushed.

"You look ready for anything," she observed, smiling. "Perhaps not marriage— not quite yet. But anything else."

I was touched by her insight. She knew me well, and knew I was a long way from being ready for marriage. At that moment I saw the flicker of something worried in her eyes. She had looked from me to Lily, and back to me again. As she looked at Lily I saw an expression of combined relief and sadness in her eyes.

"Give us a kiss," she said, holding out her arms.

Later that night some girls came over and we drank wine until midnight. There were hugs all around. The girls all admired Lily's choice. Not only was Rob from a fine family, but he had asserted his independence from that family. He was not bound by it. He was handsome, talented, and was crazy about Lily. All these things, in our opinion, made him a good match for her.

But in my heart of hearts I was still puzzled by the suddenness of Lily's decision, and by her choice of a boy she hadn't seemed serious about before. And later, as we sat together on her bed, she said something that confirmed in me my worry.

"What about you, Kate? Have you heard from Jordan?" she asked.

"No." I had lost track of Jordan completely. I had written him often at first, and he had answered a couple of times from Groton, but then his silence made me self-conscious about writing further, and I had given up.

"I wonder where he is right now," Lily said. "Tonight."

I said nothing. I assumed he was asleep if he was living in Europe, since it was five hours later there. But in my mind I saw him with a girl somewhere, wide-awake and having a fine time.

Lily had turned to look at me.

"Kate, sweetie," she said. "Remember when we were little?"

I smiled. "How little?"

"When we were too little to know better." Her wistful look surprised me. "All the messes we got into…"

"Messes, yes," I said.

Suddenly she lay back, her eyes on the ceiling where the shadow of the curtains, thrown by the streetlight outside, hung like a picture from a magic lantern.

"I used to look at the ceiling and make believe the world was upside down," she said. "The chandeliers and chairs and tables were sticking up from a white floor, and I was the one looking down from above. Sometimes I wondered why I didn't go crashing down on them. It felt so risky, just looking at the ceiling."

There was a silence.

"God help me," Lily said in a whisper. "I don't want to get into a mess."

5

* * *

It is a spring day. The sun is bright and warm, throwing spangles of light on new leaves whose undersides are still dewy. The air is fresh, the sky a deep blue. The weather seems inappropriate for a sad occasion. Forever afterward I will associate death, uncomfortably, with warm weather and sunshine.

Lily and I are attending the funeral of Peter Gracian, a boy in our class at school who has died after a year-long battle with leukemia. We girls are still small, and until now we have known death only as something that eliminates distant relatives from our lives. This includes my father, who died before I really knew him. But Peter is different. The death of a classmate brings us face-to-face with the notion that a human being we took for granted can be wiped off the face of the earth.

We attend the funeral with our families. I know everybody there except one boy, who emerges from a limousine with his mother and sits apart from the rest of us during the service. I keep looking at him because he has naturally sad eyes, and they seem to fit the occasion. He is dressed in a perfect little suit with a waistcoat, so dark that it seems made for mourning. His mother is also dressed in black, with a veil that makes it hard for me to see her face. I notice other people turning to look at them, but I don't wonder why.

After the burial there is a gathering at the home of the dead boy's parents. They have two other children, both girls, who seem annoyed by all the attention they are getting from the grown-ups. I find myself sitting next to the little boy in the three-piece suit, and I am just exerting myself to think up something to say to him when a whisper sounds behind us, urgent and demanding.

"Come with me."

I turn to see Lily with her face close to ours and a hand on each shoulder. We are both hesitant to follow her lead, but she won't take no for an answer, so we sneak out of the house with her and sit on the steps under the spring sun.

"What's your name?" Lily asks the boy.

"Jordan. Jordan Brady."

"Hi, Jordan."

"Hi."

She points to me. "This is Kate. She's my friend. How come you don't go to our school?"

"I don't know." The boy seems embarrassed.

"Where do you go?"

"Allendale," he says.

"How do you get to school? Do they have a bus?"

He shakes his head. He doesn't seem to want to answer. It will not occur to me until much later that his chauffeur probably drives him to Allendale, and that this embarrasses him.

"How come you are here?" Lily asks. "Did you know Peter?"

"My mom knows his mom," Jordan says. "I didn't know him."

"Oh." Lily sits kicking her legs out in front of her, first one and then the other. "Well, let's get out of here."

"Where are we going?" It is I who asks this. I am concerned about being punished if we wander away from such a solemn gathering.

"Just around the block," Lily says. "They'll never miss us. Come on."

We walk down the block, Lily leading the way. She is taller than I, and I am taller than Jordan. She has firm, long strides, and it is somewhat hard for us to keep up. As soon as we have rounded the corner she begins to skip. I imitate her halfheartedly.

Then she turns to Jordan.

"Kate is an orphan," she says. "She has no mom or dad."

I am a bit embarrassed to see this fact revealed to a stranger, but I sense that Lily was trying to put Jordan at his ease somehow. We continue down the block to the corner, and Lily points out a small park with a slide, a jungle gym and a merry-go-round.

"Come on," she commands.

We watch each other slide down the slide. Then Lily pushes me and Jordan on the merry-go-round. She keeps up a steady stream of conversation.

"I have two brothers and two sisters," she says. "My oldest brother, Carl, has a chemistry set. He's going to let me help him do an experiment. I hate my sister Ingrid. She's ugly."

After a while she says to me, "Kate, tell Jordan about your aunt."

"She's not much fun," I say, looking into the quiet eyes of the perplexed little boy. "She reads the Bible all the time. We don't have a TV."

"Tell us about your mother," Lily says to Jordan. Apparently my story of my aunt is too boring to suit her.

"She's nice," Jordan says loyally. "She's going to teach me to ride a horse."

Lily is pushing us with remarkable energy, and we are going around so fast that I begin to feel dizzy.

"Can we come to your house sometime?" Lily asks Jordan.

"Yes," Jordan replies.

"Let's get out of here," she says suddenly.

We tumble off the merry-go-round before it can slow to a stop, and before I completely regain my balance we are leaving the park by the opposite corner from the one we entered by. We end up on a pretty little street with very small houses. I have never seen it before.

Lily talks about her little brother and sister, and how she diapered them both and taught them to read. She tells about her father's job in town, and her family's plan to go camping in Canada in the summer. She exhibits the normal selfishness of small children, but in her sharing of so much information about herself I feel a sort of gift given to Jordan. Much later it will occur to me that perhaps she was aware, as I was not, that his situation in the society of the county was not an easy one. In her very bragging she is proving she has no secrets from him and is completely free to be his friend.

She must be distracted by her own conversation, for when we try to head back toward the dead boy's house we get lost. Jordan and I are both unnerved by this, but Lily leads the way relentlessly, stopping at corners to look this way and that, noting street names, and not showing the slightest sign of distress.

When we cut through the lawn of one of the frame houses, a huge dog appears from nowhere and chases us away with frantic barks. We run as fast as our legs can carry us. When we are out of range, still hearing the baying of the dog, Jordan and I look at each other, and at Lily. She seems a bit pale, but she is laughing. "Stupid dog. Hasn't he ever seen a kid before?"

We finally reach a tiny group of storefronts clustered around a traffic signal. Lily leads the way into a small grocery store and walks boldly up to the counter. A man with glasses and a large handlebar moustache looks down at us.

"Please, sir," Lily asks, "we're lost. We started out from Mr. and Mrs. Gracian's house, and we can't find our way back."

"Do you know what street they're on?" the man asks.

Lily looks at Jordan and me. We shake our heads.

"No, sir," she says.

"Well, let me look in the phone book." The man pulls out a small phone book with a dubious glance at us, and finds the number. "They're on Grandview," he says. "How did you get way over here?"

On his own initiative he calls the Gracians' and speaks to someone who promises to have Lily's mother pick us up. Fifteen minutes later Lily's mother drives up in her old sedan and waves to us.

"What happened?" she asks. She conceals her worry under a hospitable smile for Jordan and me.

"We took a walk and we got lost," Lily says without apologizing. "Mother, this is Jordan Brady."

"Oh, I know Jordan," Mrs. France says, surprising us girls. "Your mother is pretty worried," she tells him. "We'd better get back."

"A dog chased us," Lily volunteers as the car pulls away from the curb.

"Well, that happens," says Mrs. France with a little shrug and an amused smile.

We three children are sitting in the back seat. I turn to look at the others.

Jordan looks neat and quiet as ever in his little dark suit. My dress is rumpled, and one of my white socks has picked up a few burrs from our travels. Lily is, surprisingly, a mess. Her hair is awry, her stocking is torn, her shoes are scuffed, and there are bruises on her hands. I don't understand how this has happened. All I saw her do was push us on the merry-go-round and slide down the slide a couple of times.

"Mom?" she asks.

"Yes, sweetie."

"Can we go to Jordan's house sometime if his mother invites us?"

"Well, if Mrs. Brady invites you, I think that might be nice."

When we arrive back at the Gracians' house, Mrs. Brady is waiting outside. Her face, behind her veil, looks deeply worried, and something about the posture of her body seems fragile, breakable. She gathers Jordan to her and hugs him hard. "Oh, I was so worried about you!" she cries.

"No harm done," says Lily's

mother, putting an arm around Jordan's mother's shoulder. "They just look a little walk, and wandered too far." There is something oddly familiar about the way Mrs. France holds the other woman, as though Mrs. Brady's delicate nature is something she knows all about. I also notice, not for the first time, how much alike Lily and her mother are. Mrs. France is shrugging off our disappearance very much as Lily herself shrugged off our lostness and the dog that chased us.

"Well, all's well that ends well," she concludes. "Elizabeth, I'll call you." She bends to shake Jordan's hand. "Jordan, take good care of your mother."

Indeed, as the Brady chauffeur holds the car door open, and Jordan holds his mother's arm to help her inside, he looks for all the world like an undersized doctor escorting an invalid. I sense, with my little girl's intuition, that the dangers we encountered on our walk were nothing compared to the invisible chagrin that haunts Jordan's mother.

Before the door closes I hear him saying to her, "Mom, can Lily and Kate come over to play someday?"

And so the funeral of Peter Gracian has ended. The death of a boy I knew only slightly is eclipsed by the entry into my life of a new boy who is to become crucial to my very identity. And all because of Lily, who plucked us both from the ceremony of mourning and led us into a new adventure—the adventure of our threeness. It was Lily who chose us. I am never to forget that.

Lily and Rob's wedding went off smoothly. By the time they returned from their honeymoon in Hawaii I was already in New York. I later heard that after her first semester at the university, Lily became pregnant and dropped out. Her plan was to take courses at the local community college and get her B.A. later on, perhaps after she had finished having children.

I didn't have time to think about Lily very much in the next few years. My education in journalism was also an education in New York living, and in men.

As a girl who had grown up in the hinterlands, I was completely amazed by New York. The sheer rush of it stunned me, as did the cold confidence of the New Yorkers who shouldered their way through those crowded streets toward whatever private, unknowable destiny awaited them. These were people in a hurry, people on the move. They made a stark contrast to the people I had been with all my life, people who did little more than sit and wait for something to happen to them.

But my life as an orphan had equipped me for this loneliest of cities, where each citizen looks after himself or herself and never expects aid and comfort from others. I accepted the isolation of the city dweller as a natural condition. I hurried through my daily obligations, was friendly to those my studies put me in contact with, and kept my own counsel. I had always been a dreamer, anyway. Now I simply thickened the walls around my inner life, squared my shoulders and charged along the sidewalks of New York without letting them touch anything but the bottoms of my feet.

This attitude stood me in good stead through the four years of journalism school. When I got my degree I had doubts about my ability to compete in the crowded world of New York journalism. I hesitated, sending out applications for jobs in smaller markets. But then a professor of mine recommended me for a job with a local news magazine; a nice apartment on Seventy-first Street suddenly came available, and I was living and working in New York.

I was now dating a lot of men. I had finally outgrown my braces-and-pimples period, and was a reasonably attractive girl, with frizzy auburn hair and a sprinkling of freckles on my white cheeks. I did a certain amount of jogging, and sit-ups in front of the TV at night in my tiny apartment, but it was the constant running of my job that kept me trim. Chasing after people with a pad and pencil, it turns out, is a great way to keep in shape, if not a balm for the nerves.

Young men were interested in me. I was never sure why. Was it my quickly developed New York sophistication, combined with my provincial temperament? My thoughtfulness, which retained something wistful and out-of-place in a New Yorker? Or my humor, which, under the circumstances, had become one of my strongest weapons against the lonely nights?

I never knew. But I didn't lack for dates. Evenings at the theater came as often as I wanted. The same went for the ballet, the Philharmonic, and a lot of restaurants. New York was making room for me, after all.

Then one day an impossibly handsome young man who seemed familiar appeared at my desk and asked me, with a straight face, "Aren't you the woman they told me about?"

"What do you mean?"

"The one who came from the country?"

He was looking down at me with genuine appreciation.

"In a manner of speaking," I said. "I

grew up in a small town. A series of small towns, I should say.''

"I, too, come from the country," he said. "No civilization for a thousand miles."

"Really? Where is that?"

"Queens," he said. And just like that I recognized his accent.

"As one immigrant to another," he said, "will you have lunch with me? I'm sure we have a lot in common."

His name was Brett, and he was an editor at a rival magazine. He had a journalism degree from Columbia, but had ambitions to work in publishing. He was right in saying we had a lot in common. Between us— as I found out at that first lunch—we seemed to know just about everybody in the magazine, advertising and newspaper businesses.

Brett genuinely coveted my fish-out-of-water status in New York. He was sick of dating girls whose attitudes were all the same, and he found my introspective personality attractive.

He was hard to resist. He was an extraordinarily good-looking devil, at six-three,

with smooth brown hair and tawny, bedroom eyes. Women's heads turned to look
at him when we walked down a street or
into a restaurant together. He worked occasionally as a male model, and I amused
myself by keeping a scrapbook of his magazine layouts.

I lost my virginity with Brett, though he
didn't realize it, I think, because of a combination of my physical make-up and my
desire to hide what was happening. Why I
had remained a virgin for so long I can't
explain. I had had my opportunities. But
something made me feel I might be giving
something up before it was time—with
those other boys. By the time Brett came
along, my impatience overcame this inner
scruple. I needed to be a woman in order to
survive.

After the ice was broken, so to speak, we
kept dating and eventually moved in together. A combination of mutual sympathy
and loneliness kept us together. Brett supplied the optimism, I supplied the cooking,
and we took turns supplying the humor. We
were good companions for each other. It

was possible that that was all we would ever be, but I chose not to think about that yet. I had a man of my own. I didn't have to sleep alone anymore. In New York, this meant a lot.

During this time I heard from Lily, of course. She and Rob had two children, both girls. I came home to help out after Susie's birth, but left after less than a week, realizing that Ingrid was more than a match for the situation. When Beth was born, eighteen months later, I was on an assignment and congratulated Lily by phone.

Thanks to a loan from Rob's father not long after Lily's wedding, the France house had remained in the family. Lily, like a typical small-town wife, would drop in on her family at least once a day. She still felt a responsibility to hold the Frances together, and Rob was understanding about this, because his relationship with his own family was not an easy one.

But Rob and Lily and the girls lived in a new house Rob had built on the east side of town. It was not a fancy place, but it had five bedrooms, and one only had to look at it to realize that Rob wanted more than just two children. There was also an attic studio where Lily worked on her painting and sculpture in what was left of her spare time.

Nowadays Lily and I talked on the phone more often. Lily was her usual confident, funny self. As the headaches of motherhood overtook her, she became necessarily a bit less soft. Often she had to say "Hold on," and then her voice would call a warning to one of the children, *"Stop doing that to her!"* or *"I told you to put that down!"* But she adored both girls. Seeing her with them often brought a pulse of wistful envy to me. She had all a mother's skills. Warmth, confidence, loving discipline, humor.

I could see this was going to be her great achievement in life, and it always made me a bit uncomfortable when, as "Aunt Kate," I visited. I didn't feel complete as a woman, compared to Lily. With her fingers stained by jelly, her hair tied back in a ponytail to avoid messes, her eyes tired from running after two kids all day long, she looked amazingly feminine. I, in my immaculate New York outfits, with my makeup and journalist's hair, felt like a soulless mannequin next to her.

Ironically, she was no longer as impatient with my nostalgia as she had been when we were in high school. Nowadays, as she sat holding one of her girls in her arms, it was Lily who would evoke the past in our languid afternoon conversations.

"Do you remember the time we went skinny-dipping at Fishers Pond?" she asked.

"Oh, yes." I laughed. "I think about it every time I get in the shower. What a miracle it was we didn't get caught!"

Or again, "Kate, do you remember the time we sneaked Daddy's car out of the garage and drove all the way to Huntsville?"

Of course I remembered. I was only surprised that she cared enough to bring up the old adventures. I would have been happy to dilate on them with her, but the cloudy wistfulness in her eyes disappeared as she looked down at her daughter. It was as though she could only give the old moment a brief second of her attention before the claims of the present eclipsed it. Nevertheless I sensed that I was now a link to a past that mattered to her. She counted on me to keep the torch alive.

One day the clock turned abruptly backward and the old Lily reappeared for a moment. We were all standing in the kitchen, and Lily had her hand down the disposal, trying to extricate a piece of stuck food. She had narrow hands with long, limber fingers, and was adept at fiddling in tight places like car engines and sewing machines.

Just as she was struggling with the disposal, a very large spider crawled along the countertop. The girls screamed in alarm. Rob turned to get a paper towel, but the spider was moving quickly toward a corner where it could escape under the sink. As Rob hesitated, Lily cried, "Get it, you sissy!" And, with one quick motion, she pulled her wet hand from the disposal and crushed the spider under her fingers.

"Yuck," she said, shaking the squashed spider into the wastebasket. Then she smiled sheepishly at Rob, who was still holding the now-useless paper towel, an amazed look on his face. "Sorry. I got carried away."

I was struck less by her impatience with her husband than by the fact that for a brief instant the old Lily had appeared among us, fearless, with dirty hands, leading the way and very impatient with those who followed in her trail. That was the Lily I once knew so well, and missed. Fugitive as a bloom of fireworks against the sky, she had shared herself with us and then disappeared, hidden under the quiet adult woman who had taken her place. I took comfort in the thought that she was not entirely gone.

Thus our friendship endured, forced by time to adapt itself to new circumstances, but with one foot in the past. I had finger paintings by Lily's children on my refrigerator. I sent them gifts for their birthdays, and they scrawled thank-you notes with crayons or pencils. I spoke to them on the phone when I talked to Lily. She sent me snapshots. And always, somewhere underneath the new years and the new skin needed to live in them, she remained my

Lily. My other half, my witness, my secret twin.

She never came to New York, but I went back "home" when I could find the time. My trips gave me a feeling of having roots (which no New Yorker ever really has), and even a sense of direction. As "Aunt Kate" I was still part of a family. And as Lily's friend—best friend, still—I had an identity. Somehow everything that had happened in New York, including Brett, had not supplied this.

The years passed without my bothering to count them. Then one evening my phone rang, and I heard a voice that was difficult to place at first.

"Kate? This is your—this is Carl France."

My body went rigid. I had never spoken to Carl on the phone in my life. *Lily is dead, I thought.*

"I'm sorry to call you this late at night," Carl said. "The fact is—well, our mother died today."

I couldn't find any words. Carl was saying something about Lily being out with other family members, and telling me about the funeral arrangements. Mrs. France's death did not come as a surprise. Her heart condition had had her virtually bedridden for the last few years. But I was stricken by the news. Having reconciled myself to the sad fact that her illness was terminal, I had fooled myself into thinking that her decline would simply go on forever. I had forgotten that one day she would simply not be there anymore. Today was that day. An unfinished letter to her was in my computer even as Carl spoke.

I flew up from New York for the funeral. The effect of the loss on the family was already obvious. Mr. France seemed dazed and unbelieving. In his dark suit and tie, talking with the pastor, he looked like a ghost.

"Hello, Kate," said Ingrid, coming up to put her plump arms around me. "It was good of you to come."

"This isn't easy," I said. "She was the only real mother I ever had."

I remembered the way Mrs. France had

greeted me as "my prodigal daughter" every time I came up from New York. She knew all about Brett, and all about my work. More than once I had felt her sharp mind weighing my words as I told her about my choices in life. But she had never been disapproving in this. She just wanted to make sure I was getting my best chance for happiness.

"I know, dear," said Ingrid. "We're all going to miss her. She was the one who kept us a family." She glanced at the others behind her. "I'm not sure what will happen now."

It was obvious to me that Mrs. France had been everything to Ingrid, who was confirmed in her spinsterhood and would never have a life of her own. I was touched to see how bravely she took over the reins as hostess, to bury the very woman she had served with such fidelity and patience all these years.

As for Carl, whom I greeted next, he didn't seem to remember having phoned me. He looked more shattered than anyone by the loss of his mother. He spent most of his time in his third-floor "office," and when we were all together for a meal or a conversation, he kept his teeth clenched. The look in his eyes was that of a man who is falling through ice and trying to seem casual about it. I looked away.

Christine, the younger sister, was there with her boyfriend. She greeted me with surprising warmth, considering the fact that I had seen very little of her in the past few years.

"Kate, I want you to meet my boyfriend," she said. "Gary, this is Kate. You've heard all about her."

A somewhat nondescript but smiling individual shook my hand. He was one of a series of boyfriends Christine had brought home since her divorce. She had married a local boy from a good family, but there had been infidelity on both sides, and the marriage had ended in less than two years. Now she was drifting in and out of town, dating a series of men who all seemed to have in common their rootlessness and their lack of serious "prospects."

She was still pretty, though the years had

taken away some of her freshness. She showed no emotion about her mother's death. She asked me about life in New York, and about Brett, with a coldly attentive look in her eyes, as though thinking that New York might offer her the marital future she had so far failed to attain.

No one had been able to find Eric. He had moved to California years before, and not bothered to keep the family informed of his current address.

Rob had finished his law degree, but changed his mind and agreed to go to work for his father. He now did all the legal work for the Sewell businesses, and in his spare time took care of the Frances' finances. He was very considerate to me, apparently realizing how much Mrs. France had meant to me. I also saw him taking the time to talk to Carl and Mr. France. Clearly Rob had become the strong male in the family, as Lily was the strong woman.

I found myself alone with Lily in my room late the night after the funeral. I was to go back to the city early the next morning. I had watched Lily kiss the children good-night. She seemed like her usual self, but softened a bit by the grief around her, and by the obvious fact that, with Mrs. France dead, it would now fall to her to supply the warmth, the good cheer, the courage that sets the tone for a happy family when unhappiness is snapping at its heels, as is always the case in this world.

We sat drinking white wine and talking. Lily looked tired. After a while I noticed she had something in her hand.

"What's that?" I asked.

She looked down at the object, as though scrutinizing it for the answer to a private riddle. Then she handed it to me. It was a faded old photograph, printed on thick cardboard.

"It's a picture of Jordan's father," she said. "I found it under the lining of Mother's jewelry box."

I recognized the handsome face of Mr. Brady without difficulty. As I looked at the strong chin, the aquiline nose, I thought of Jordan and wondered whether he had grown up to look like this. Then I realized that something about the picture was different. I closed my eyes and searched my memory for those long-ago days when this face was familiar. Then I looked again, and realized that in this photo Mr. Brady was not wearing his patented smile. His face was serious, and something tender and vulnerable had replaced his usual arrogance.

Images of Lily's mother flashed before my mind's eye, confused as shards of glass in a kaleidoscope. I saw the look on Mrs. France's face when Jordan's father was mentioned. I thought of her friendship with Mrs. Brady, which lasted so many years, her loyalty to the crazed woman when all others were forsaking her.

Could there have been something about my beloved "mother" that I never knew? Was there something about all of us that I still did not understand?

I was too tired to pursue this trend of thought. Again I looked at Lily's face, which was now sculpted by grief into something almost unrecognizable.

"You know," I said, "you and Rob ought to get away for a while. Let Ingrid take care of the kids. Or even hire someone. Just a few days. Maybe a resort. Just be alone together for a while.''

''He's having an affair.''

I almost asked ''Who?'' but stopped myself in time.

There was a quiet, hard look in Lily's eyes that I had never seen before. Only now did I realize how much her cheerfulness the last few days must have cost her.

''Do you know who it is?'' I managed to say at last.

''Some woman he met at work,'' she said. ''It doesn't matter.''

I told myself stupidly that at least it was not some old flame he had never gotten over. Then I felt the brute insistence of the truth, and saw it in the nervous way Lily twisted her glass.

I sensed that this was one of those times in life when one misfortune piles on another, but I was not prepared for her next words.

''I'm pregnant again.''

She was silent after this, as though bitterly satisfied that her abrupt statement of her dilemma needed no further elaboration.

I said nothing for a long moment. I knew I'd turned red, but she wasn't looking at me.

"Does he know?" I asked.

She tossed her head in a gesture that could have meant yes, no, or I don't care.

Then I asked, "Are you going to have it?"

She nodded. She seemed resigned, but also determined. I got the sense that she was living a life she had chosen, and would not let even a thing like her husband's infidelity interfere with it.

"Lily..."

She shook her head slowly, then looked up at me. Tears were in her eyes.

"Oh, Kate, my mom is dead."

She began to cry in silence. She made no attempt to dry her tears. I had never seen her look so desolate.

I removed the wineglass from her hand and took her in my arms. She curled on her side so that her head was in my lap.

For a long time I tried to think of something to say. Then I gave up. What came to my lips was not a sentence, but a song.

> Little sparrow, it's September.
> Winter's coming, you can't stay.
> When you're gone will you remember
> All the games we used to play?

> Night is dark, the bells are ringing,
> You've been gone since yesterday.
> In my dream I hear you singing,
> Little sparrow, far away.

This was the lullaby that Mrs. France used to sing when she came in to kiss me good-night. The song was sad, but Mrs. France's soft voice seemed to put a smile into the words. And the bird's departure, after all, promised a return in the spring, though a child's imagination has difficulty with such long absences. I sang it in a murmur, savoring the memories it evoked. As I held Lily's head in my lap, caressing her hair as Mrs. France had once caressed mine, I felt the years drift away like sheets of paper in a breeze, and the old warmth of home flowed through me into my voice and my fingers.

A sob escaped her lips.

"Yes, dear heart," I said. "No one can hear us. Go on."

She cried for a long time. I held her until I felt her grief ebb to somnolence. She had had little sleep these past days, with the children to look after and the guests, and her siblings being so little help in any spiritual sense. I felt my own lonely past calling out its response, scar for scar, throb for throb, though it was only tonight I had realized what my friend was going through in life.

After a while she got up with a sigh and said she had to go to bed. She turned at the doorway and gave me a long, tired hug, resting her head on my shoulder.

"You're the one who knew me when," she said. And with those words echoing in my ear with a sudden heartbreaking sound, she walked away from me.

I was getting ready to go to bed, and fighting back my own tears, when I noticed the photograph of Jordan's father on the dresser. I picked it up. Underneath it was a crumpled piece of paper. Lily must have brought it in with her before.

It was a telegram. The fold obscured most of the message, but I could see a few of the words.

...a mother to me, too. I will never forget her...

I unfolded the page to peek at the sender's name. My eyes opened wide, though I was not entirely surprised.

The telegram was from Jordan Brady.

6

Lily miscarried her third child—a boy—and had no more children. She did not divorce Rob. I never heard whether there was a confrontation over his infidelity or not. The next time I visited she was her old self. She didn't mention our nocturnal conversation in the wake of her mother's death, and I got the clear message that she didn't want me to broach it, either.

Nor did she mention the telegram she left by accident in my room, or the photo she found in her mother's jewelry box. I knew these things had been significant to her, but I had the strong feeling they were not to be discussed.

The next few years were busy ones for me. I managed to develop a reputation as a skilled author of profiles, and more and more of my time was spent doing in-depth articles, as long as fifty thousand words, on major figures in the business and financial world. I branched out to the arts—which was not easy in a city overloaded with music, theater and art critics—and in the end I had more work than I could handle.

I was a confirmed New Yorker now. I belonged—as much as anyone else, anyway. Yet I was rootless. The city was not a place where you put down roots. The soil could not support them, for it was too covered with decades' worth of steel and concrete and ambition. It was a place you negotiated, an obstacle course. A place where you "got ahead." That's why everyone was always in such a hurry.

Eventually, despite my conviction that I was happy, this life began to wear on me. And ultimately the process of erosion brought an end to my relationship with Brett. He had proposed to me several times and been asked to wait. In the end he gave up. The final conversation took place in a restaurant high above the city, with Brett hemming and hawing, at a loss for words for the first time in his life, and me holding his hand and encouraging him to say what I knew he had come to say.

The next day he moved his things out of my apartment, and it was done. We shook hands, both sweaty from the exertion of the moving, and I looked at him affectionately.

"Do you realize," I said, "that we've been together for seven years? That's longer than most marriages."

He smiled. "I never thought of it that way. Perhaps we should have a bottle of champagne on it."

We did. And that was the end. I saw him occasionally in the old places—New York is a very small town to those who have friends there—and, a year later, I attended his wedding. He married a girl he had known as a teenager in Queens, a divorcée now. I wished them well.

My shoulders were squared; I was ready for the future, whatever it might bring. I suspected there would be a long hiatus before another man came into my life. Indeed, there might never be another one.

I was wrong.

I came across Jordan Brady's name in my travels as a journalist. He had made a name for himself in business, apparently through some brilliant real-estate dealings, and his name was mentioned occasionally in the financial press. He owned a lot of properties, both here and abroad, and divided his time between London and New York, where he maintained an apartment in the East Sixties.

A dozen times I thought about getting in touch with him. Each time I vetoed the idea, perhaps because so much time had passed, and perhaps because of the rejection I had felt when he stopped answering my letters back in high school. I suspected I would run into him, as one always runs into people in New York. I rehearsed what I would say to him.

"Fancy meeting you here."

"Small world."

"Do you know who I am?"

It was this last question, and the fear that he would not remember, that decided me definitively not to seek him out. But the thought of him forced me to realize that there was more to my dissatisfaction in those days than the exile of New York. Adult life had disappointed me in another way, a way I did not willingly admit to myself.

I had never stopped thinking about Jordan, and about Lily and me. I remembered the fever of our closeness—our ''threeness''—and our boundless hope. Somehow the violence of our parting—the suicide of Jordan's mother, the economic crash, the abrupt end of our world—had preserved intact, like an insect in amber, my dream of belonging to a thing eternal, a thing sanctified and beautiful that burned so intensely that it could defy time. And the number defining that mystic flame was three.

Perhaps it was because I had been an orphan all my life, until Lily and Jordan came along. I'll probably never understand it entirely. In any case, our time together remained a standard against which I measured my adult experience. And that experience always fell short. This might have influenced my decision to refuse Brett's proposals of marriage. It was as though I was still trying to hold myself intact, to offer myself pure, for something greater than what life had yet offered me.

I never consciously admitted this to myself—I would have been ashamed, as a hard-bitten adult, to do so—but I came back to it silently, in the dead of night, when my day was over and I waited for sleep. It was a refuge. And as the loss of Brett sank into me, I found myself clinging to this inner torch as a protection against the new sting of my loneliness. With Brett gone I was alone again, twenty-eight years old, and more of an orphan than ever. It comforted me to think of the one time in my life when, with Lily and Jordan in my arms, I had felt that loneliness was an impossibility. It seemed a sin to linger over something so strictly forbidden by time as well as reality, but I gave in to it, anyway.

My aunt Clara, the last of the senile aunts to have been my guardian, died not long after I broke up with Brett. I had never been close to her, really, and I might not even have gone to her funeral had I not recalled that some of my "stuff" was stored in her attic in Oregon.

I felt an impulse to put my life in order in the wake of losing Brett, so I flew there and stayed a couple of days in Clara's smelly old house, commiserating with distant relatives who seemed confused about who I was. The experience was unpleasant for the very reason that it touched me so little. I felt almost nothing. Yet my past was slipping through my fingers for good.

These conflicting emotions must have been inside me when I went up into Clara's attic to look for my things. There were two large boxes. A few old dresses, some books, a pair of dancing shoes.

Then I found a notebook I had once bought with the good intention of making it my journal. There were only a handful of entries before the vast bulk of blank pages attested to my abandoning the diary idea.

But pressed between two of these pages was a photograph of Jordan and Lily in their fancy dress from the night of the ball, now so many years ago. I was astonished at how young they looked. Lily seemed taller than Jordan, and he had the face of a boy. The background was annihilated by the professional photographer's flash, but their faces stood out shining with youth, and I could clearly see the excitement that had possessed them that night.

Along with the picture there was the corsage Jordan's butler had delivered to me that day, the corsage I had not worn to the ball, because I didn't go. But I had saved it lovingly, and now, dried out and crumbling, it testified to the self I had once been and, more important, the trio of which I had been a member.

I looked at the back of the photo. It bore the message, *BP from PF*. "Bottomless Pit" from "Pink Fingers." And the date, which seemed a lifetime ago.

I held the two artifacts in my hands. I closed my eyes and recalled my conversation with Stanford, the butler, in the garden as I watched Jordan and Lily from a distance. I recalled our meeting on the golf course in the wee hours, and our exultation as we clung to each other in the shadow of impending separation. I felt something quicken inside me, like a forbidden impulse, in response to the memory of all that childish emotion.

And then, all at once, I remembered. The rendezvous.

It was on that night, June 14, the three of us thirteen years old, that we had promised to meet fifteen years later, on our favorite hole on Jordan's father's overgrown golf course. The Fertile Crescent.

The fifteen years had passed. It was now June 6. There were eight days to go until the rendezvous.

I thought about our old promise during my trip back to New York. It occurred to me to send lighthearted letters or faxes to Jordan and Lily, perhaps reminding them in cryptic terms of the importance of next Friday. But I did not want to test them in that way. I realized the old promise came from another world. It spoke to me alone. It would have been unfair to impose it on my old friends.

By the time I arrived at my Seventy-first Street apartment, emptied now of all traces of Brett (except a single pair of tennis shoes), I had made up my mind. The next morning I began rearranging my schedule for the next week.

The night before the appointed day I lay in my bed from eight o'clock until midnight, thinking. I was not sure what my intention was. I realized in some vague way that nothing could happen, no one would be there. But I was going to do this for myself. I was going to confront the past and, if possible, turn a page on it. For at the moment I felt I was not doing justice to my future; I needed to open doors I myself could not see clearly enough.

The next morning I took a cab to La-Guardia and flew to Boston, where I took a commuter flight to Portland. I rented a car and drove the rest of the way to Summer Harbor. I arrived in town at about four in the afternoon. I had already decided not to call at Lily's house and tell her why I was here.

I avoided the village, for I knew there were people in town who knew me and might approach me. I drove to the old Brady house just to make sure it was still there. I remembered Lily telling me that someone had paid up the property taxes and the mortgage so the place couldn't be repossessed.

The house had not changed. It sparkled in the June sunshine. As always, its decay was hidden by distance. It seemed like a talisman, defying time. I could look at it and see myself at a dozen different moments of my life. The night of Mrs. France's funeral, the night before Lily's wedding, the night of the ball and of our promise—the house was the center around which the kaleidoscope of our years had turned. I sensed an obscure danger in this, but it did not scare me away. The contrary, in fact.

The golf course was still there, looking not much more overgrown than it had all those years ago. Apparently Nature had exhausted her efforts to completely reclaim the land in the first few years after Brady Sr.'s death, and then given up.

I drove around the county as the afternoon waned, looking at various sights from the past, including the fish hatchery and the county park where Lily and Jordan and I

used to swim together. I got out of the car
and sat on a picnic table, staring at nothing.

I was waiting for night. The rendezvous
should take place after dark, I thought, like
our promise itself.

It was daylight saving time, and dusk was
slow to come to the town. I began to get
itchy. I felt I was doing something crazy in
coming here—and doing it alone. My trip
would end up as a painful confirmation of
my exile in life. The more so because I had
not learned to live in the present, but had
journeyed here in the laborious pursuit of a
past that was completely gone.

Finally the sun began to set. I drove
across town to Jordan's house. Once dusk
had begun it seemed to accelerate. The light
faded quickly. I parked the car in the old
driveway by the postern and had to rush to
reach the appointed place before the or-
ange-drenched sky turned dark.

I lost my way, to my surprise. The trees
seemed different, thicker, and the old path-
ways were strange. I couldn't seem to find
the thirteenth tee. Time, I realized, had

made more changes in me than I had bargained for.

Then, stumbling out of a brambled path that had once been a lane for golf carts, I saw it. The familiar canopy of oaks was much taller now, the grass dry, cattails nodding in the slight breeze. The old tee markers were gone, probably stolen by local children as trophies for their bedrooms.

The moon was rising, pale and stricken, over the ocean. I hurried forward, haunted by the foolish idea that I might be late and miss my chance for the rendezvous.

Finally I stood in the center of the tee, looking at the distant water and trying to catch my breath. I felt more than a little ridiculous. I also felt, suddenly, terribly lonely and abandoned. I was more an orphan than ever before, in this forsaken place.

I wanted to leave now, to get back in the car and hurry home. But I had no real home. That, indeed, was why I was here.

I heard a sound in the grass behind me, but I didn't think it could be a person until I heard the voice.

"Lily, is that you?"

I turned quickly. A man was coming toward me in the gloom.

"Jordan?"

"Kate?"

"Yes."

I couldn't see his face. The shadows thrown by the thick trees were too dark. But, in the adult male voice, I recognized Jordan, anyway.

"So you came," he said.

"And you."

We walked out of the shadows and saw each other's faces. He was tall now, of course, and dark. I couldn't make him out entirely—the light wasn't sufficient—but I could see that he had grown into a handsome man. I caught a glimpse of those sad gentle eyes, and they warmed me with the knowledge that all things in life don't change and die away.

"It's been a long time."

"I thought I would be the only one here."

"Me, too."

There was a long, embarrassed pause.

"What have you been doing all this time?" he asked.

I began to answer, shyly, self-deprecating as a person at a cocktail party. The story of my life sounded clumsy and commonplace on my lips. He listened in silence. When I told him I had seen his name in the papers, he told me he had finished his education at Harvard Business School, but started his career in Europe, working for some venture capitalists based in the Netherlands. "One thing led to another," he said. "I live in New York now—most of the time. It's the easiest." He seemed calmer than I was, but sad, too.

There was a pause. He looked around him at the golf course. There was a strange look in his eyes, as though the whole place was something he didn't quite understand, but with which he was obsessed. I have seen men look in that way at women they love, women who are cruel to them.

"One of the first things I did when I started making money," he said, "was to pay off the taxes on all this so they couldn't tear it down. It was a burden for the first few years. But I'm glad I kept it.''

He turned to me. ''I'm sorry I haven't written in all these years,'' he said. ''I should have looked you up. I meant to.''

''Me, too,'' I said. ''A dozen times I was going to call you.'' I laughed. ''I was afraid you wouldn't remember me.''

''That was wrong of you. Of course I would have remembered.'' There was something offended in his tone.

We said a few more things, each one a bit more lame than the last. The significance of our presence here was beginning to cancel out conversation. Something at once restful and troubling reduced us to silence. We both looked at the empty golf course stretching into the night sky.

''How did you remember?'' I asked.

''Remember what?''

''Our plan. Our date. For tonight. I was sure I would be the only one here.''

''I never forgot,'' he said in a quiet voice that shocked me by its conviction.

''Really,'' I said. ''That's amazing.''

He seemed to ponder for a moment.

"Do you see Lily?" he asked.

"Yes. Pretty often."

"How is she?"

I took an instant too long to reply. "She's fine." Then, on an impulse, "She has two children. Girls."

"I'm glad." I thought I saw him wince, but it may have been a trick of the moonlight.

"Mrs. France died," I added. "But perhaps you knew that."

He did not answer this.

There was another silence, this one more painful than the last. There was so much to say, so much to try to grasp. But the past slithered away like smoke. Not only all the years we had lived apart, but our promise itself. It seemed wrong, incredibly wrong, that we were here. A crazy contradiction. A sin against time, as it were.

And Lily was not here. With each passing minute we felt that more acutely. We had dared to turn back the clock and act out the wishes of our childish selves. Lily had not. She had not remembered. How could she? Adults don't remember the wishes of children they have long since left behind.

Or if she had remembered, she had dismissed the old promise as any adult would, no doubt assuming, in her practicality, that no one else would be here. After all, the rendezvous place was right in her own town, and must seem far less magical to her than to Jordan and I, who were so far removed from it by distance as well as the years.

"She still lives here," I said with unconscious cruelty. His nod told me I was not telling him something he didn't already know.

He took my remark as an opening, and asked me questions about Lily, her marriage, her daughters, the surviving Frances. He seemed to devour every word I said. I realized that the past was, for reasons I could not know, even more alive in him than in myself.

"Just think," I said at last, "she's right out there in the darkness, not five minutes away."

"And fifteen years," Jordan said. "One

of my professors used to remind us that our existence is bounded by time as well as space. Every day he would give us another example of it. 'Do you see the student sitting in the seat in front of you? Imagine a huge hand appearing from nowhere and snatching that student away. Well, that hand is already here. It's called time. An hour from now, a semester from now that student will not be sitting there. He or she will be gone.' We laughed. He told us not to. 'You won't find it so funny when it's your wife or husband, or your child that is being taken away from you,' he said.''

Jordan looked at the stars, which were coming out shyly in the young night sky, like handmaidens to the moon. ''Remember the old philosophical riddle about the tree that falls in the woods when there's no one there to see or hear it?''

I nodded. ''Whether the tree is real or not,'' I said.

''That same professor told us we would do better to wonder whether we ourselves are real, since we'll be gone so soon.'' He shrugged. ''I saw what he meant, but I

never thought it was important. Now I do
see.''

He meant that Lily would not come. I felt
his sadness all the more acutely because I
knew now that he had firmly expected her
to be here.

The minutes passed. Jordan and I were
joined by our awareness of the absurdity of
our childish hopes for this night. And yet,
the more we talked, the more we began to
feel a sort of stubborn alliance between us.
We knew we looked ridiculous standing
here under the moonlight in search of a lost
dream, but we had at least made the trip.
We had defied the years.

And somehow this shared defiance
brought our childhood selves timidly forward to join hands with the adults we had
become. Something playful and mischievous came over us, and I remembered those
precious afternoons when we children
roamed these hills, drunk with our own initiative and convinced that everything the
eye could see belonged to us, and not to the
adults who thought they owned it.

We sat down in the thick grass. The

moon rose higher and higher. The more brightly it lit the scene, the more years it seemed to strip away. We talked about our old adventures, about the pranks we used to play on Jordan's mother's servants. We talked about our games, our hide-and-seek and blindman's bluff, our wanderings around town under the disapproving eyes of adults who suspected we were up to some sort of foolishness, or who were simply jealous of our happiness.

Inevitably we got around to our memory of the ball and our promise to meet here. I mentioned Lily's dress, and told Jordan about the picture I had found in Aunt Clara's attic.

"I never had a feeling like that again," Jordan said.

"What feeling do you mean?" I asked, leaning forward.

"The feeling of wanting something so much, so completely," he said, "and be-lieving that if you wanted it that much, it would have to come true."

"Yes." I could not say more. I knew this was precisely what I had lost in life—the ability to believe, to fling oneself joyously at life in the certainty that life would break your fall, would never let you down, never shatter your dreams. I was astonished to hear Jordan put my own thoughts into words so clearly.

I thought suddenly of Lily, of her struggles over the years. Perhaps it was her own way of dealing with them that had made it impossible for fate or chance to get through to her and make her remember tonight. But Jordan and I had somehow had made room in our adult selves for the old dream. And so we had remembered.

But I had remembered only at the last moment, while Jordan had never forgotten at all. I could not resist the fanciful thought that it was the intensity of Jordan's conviction that had got through to me in Oregon and reminded me of this night, and of my promise. This idea restored all my belief in him, and in the part of myself he had brought here tonight to give back to me. Tonight we were only two, but our "three-ness" was alive once more, because Jordan had refused to let it die. He had carried the torch.

When he put his arms around me, I felt a pulse of fear. But our pact overcame that. I drew him down on the grass with me, and we embraced under the watching moon. It was all sweet and strange and restful, because he had come back to me. I didn't even feel self-conscious when my body came free for him, because I knew he believed in me in a way that overcame my imperfections just as it overcame the years. He looked down at me. His eyes were hidden in the shadows, but I sensed his exultation and his relief, replacing the look of painful obsession he had worn earlier. His dream was real enough to have brought another human being to this place. He was satisfied.

After that we were a man and a woman, and the past was necessarily eclipsed by the communion of our flesh. But I never stopped feeling, in every caress, his conviction that time was no match for us, not tonight. It was only when the last wave was coming, and thought was giving way completely to the heat joining us, that I remembered his first words in the darkness tonight, when he had made me out and called to me. It was Lily's name that had been on his lips, not my own.

7

When I was small I once had an illustrated book about a little girl who encountered a benevolent but whimsical fairy godmother or witch, and was given a magical hourglass. Every time she turned the hourglass over, time itself was reversed.

The child was playful, and she turned the glass over many times. Like Alice in Wonderland, who grew suddenly larger or smaller depending on which magical potion she consumed, the little girl was transformed by each turn of the glass. She hurtled forward into her adult years, then rushed back into childhood. In the end it became almost impossible to be sure which way the sands were flowing.

The book got lost somewhere in my travels among my many relatives. I might have had it when I lived with Lily; I can't remember. When I was much older I searched for it in public libraries, bibliographies, even rare-book shops. I couldn't remember the title, so I never found the book.

But I never forgot that strange and powerful idea of time running forward and backward and forward again in a dizzying randomness. I came to feel that this was one of human time's secrets, and a great joke on us. We think time is running in an orderly course, always toward the future. We make our plans based on the assumption that time is a sort of playing field for our initiative. Tomorrow is our fetish, our only religion.

But it isn't really so. The adult person we think we have become can suddenly be thrown abruptly back into the fevered mind of the child we thought we had left behind long ago. And at that moment it is the child who rules. I suspect that, in the silence of my sleep, my own hourglass turns, mixing the sand of the present with that of the past. The forbidden doors open, the forgotten feelings burst out like goblins on Halloween, and I am back with Lily again, where my true self was created.

In some strange way Lily and Jordan and I must have suspected this secret of time when we made our promise. We were hardly out of our childhood, and clearly no match for the march of historical time, which was to separate us so completely. But our promise called out to the hidden hourglass to come to our aid, even if only on a day so distant that we might not remember our pact. And it worked. Jordan and I found our way through the tangled years to the Fertile Crescent, which was waiting for us, barely changed.

This was not the final turn, however. I was to learn the rules of this dangerous game, and the penalty for breaking them.

After the night of the promised rendez-vous I went back to my own life as though nothing had happened. The only difference was that, for now, I stopped worrying about the lack of a man in my life. After Brett, I had wondered if I would become a typical New York spinster, a ''career girl.'' Now that concern was gone. I had a warm glow inside me that took away my feelings of exile. It sounds odd to say it, but I felt I had outwitted the world somehow. I had gained something I never expected to have, and could keep with me from now on.

I never called Jordan. In fact, it didn't even occur to me to call him, though we lived in the same city. I felt that what had happened between us was as though inserted into a gap in time, like a flower inserted in a book. I certainly did not feel I had any claim to his attention, much less his love. As a matter of fact, the memory of my rendezvous with him was all the sweeter for my knowledge that he had his own life and would never see me again. I knew that, wherever he was, he remembered. That was enough.

I kept working. I still enjoyed the bustle of New York, but I moved to a roomier place on Staten Island, an apartment with two bedrooms and a real, life-size kitchen (an impossibility in Manhattan). I worked hard, but I developed a new sense of home for myself. I enjoyed being inside my own four walls. I cooked, I grew plants, I shopped for nice furniture.

Years passed. I was feeling more secure than I had ever felt before—at least, since my days with Lily and Jordan.

Then one day I got a surprising assignment. It was from *The New Yorker*, a profile article, fifty thousand words—on none other than Jordan Brady.

Jordan had become quite famous. He had branched out from real estate into other areas, including broadcast journalism and cable television, and was enormously wealthy. Because of his youth and good looks, he was often talked about as a potential political candidate.

For some time he had been on the list of America's most eligible bachelors. But now he was engaged to a young Swiss heiress, the sister of one of his classmates in prep school. She was twenty-five; Jordan was thirty-one.

I called Jordan, who knew about the plan and had agreed to it. He asked me to meet him in the afternoon at his apartment on Central Park. I tried hard to make believe the interview was just a job, but I couldn't help buying a new outfit for the occasion.

I was astonished, as a New Yorker, by the sheer size of the apartment. It must have been three or four thousand square feet, bedroom after bedroom, salon after salon, and all with a spectacular sixth-floor view of the park. I had heard that places like this existed on the Upper East Side, but I had never seen one, not even as a reporter.

Jordan greeted me at the door and took me into a solarium where his fiancée was waiting. She was a friendly, light-complected woman, surprisingly tall when she stood up to be introduced to me. She came forward with firm strides to shake my hand. He called her Chris. Her name was Christine de La Haye. Jordan did not introduce me as an old friend, only as a journalist.

Something about her manner struck me, but I could not put my finger on it. A girlish agility, a readiness for fun, which belied her European urbanity. I asked her whether she had known Jordan a long time, and she said yes, "since I was a little girl and my brother brought him home for a vacation."

They held hands as we talked, but they were not demonstrative. I learned that her family's money came from manufacturing, and that she had been educated at the Sorbonne and at Cambridge. She was an art historian, and had written articles about Renaissance painting as well as primitive art. Her manner of speech made it clear she was an intellectual of the European type, well-spoken but not opinionated. I liked her. Despite her foreignness, something about her seemed very familiar.

"I've heard a lot about your family and your childhood," I said to Jordan, "but most of it in the form of wild rumors. Perhaps you could clear it up for me."

"Sure," Jordan said, sitting with his hand in Christine's. "There's not much to tell. I come from a long line of cheap crooks and robber barons. The crooks were on my father's side of the family—Irish immigrants—and the robber barons were my mother's side. It was an unusual marriage. I don't think he would have even met her had it not been for a stroke of chance. He had a scheme for some public transportation facilities in Europe, and he was trying to line up investors in New England. One of them was her father.

"My father conceived a passion for this daughter of the rich, and managed to sweep her off her feet and get her to elope with him. He was quite a lady-killer, from what I've heard. Here, let me show you something."

He went into the next room and returned with a tiny framed photograph of a man whose smile I recognized. He wore a somewhat ill-fitting suit, and held a hat in his hand at a rakish and rather silly angle.

"That's my dad," Jordan said. "The picture doesn't do him justice. From what I hear he was very handsome and very charming. He had tremendous energy. I think my mother was a bit afraid of that energy, but also seduced by it."

There was a pause. He seemed to measure his words.

"That charm of his was apparently his chief weapon in business," he said. "Without speaking a word of any language but English, he managed to find investors in several European countries. He was planning to branch out to the Far East, as well, but he overextended himself in numerous ways. Let's just say that he lacked the stability to match his charm. After a while he lost all his money. He disappeared, and my mother never saw him again.''

''Do you think you inherited any of his qualities?'' I asked.

He laughed. ''Not the charm. At least, not that I can see. But I'm more successful than he was—so far, anyway. And I think that's because I'm less impulsive. I don't try to change the world overnight. Also, I don't try to bowl people over. I let them contribute what they want to. I like to foster a climate of cooperation. People think of me as a peacemaker, a mediator, rather than a mover and shaker.''

He was clearly wrong about the charm. Sitting with his hand in that of his fiancée and his eyes on me, he had a quiet attractiveness that was almost hypnotic. But I decided not to press the point.

"You're known for your cautiousness, financially, as well as your vision," I said. "Do you think this has something to do with wanting to avoid your father's mistakes?"

He seemed thoughtful. "Probably. I'm not sure we ever erase the imprint of our parents."

He leaned forward. "Do you remember the parable of the painter," he asked, "who painted a thousand pictures of a thousand different subjects—and when they were all put together they made a picture of his own face?"

I nodded.

"Well," he said, "that's always fascinated me. I think it's true. But I also think the picture might have been of his father's face, or his mother's face, or both. Life is really a riddle. We think we're making free decisions as we move forward in the world. Being an individual. Growing more and more like ourselves. But often it turns out that there is a secret pattern behind the whole thing that has been coloring the picture for us all along. Without realizing it, we may be struggling to reconcile ourselves with key people in our past. The struggle can take a lifetime."

He smiled. "We're never as alone as we think." I thought I saw him give me a significant look as he said this.

"Do you mean to say that your own success has been an attempt to redeem your father's failures?" I asked.

He smiled. "You're very perceptive," he said. "Yes, I think there's some truth to that. It was hard to assimilate—what happened to him. As a boy I felt, or must have felt, that he could accomplish anything. I couldn't imagine anything that could limit him. He had married my mother over the objections of her family. He had built us an enormous house. He had wealthy and influential friends, many of them famous, who visited us all the time. Then, overnight, it all ended. Yes, I'm sure that left a mark on me. Perhaps, through my own financial success, I'm trying to restore a feeling of security that was taken away at an early age."

"And how did your mother take it?" I asked. "The end of the marriage, I mean."

This time his pause was longer. He was obviously uncomfortable. I saw Christine glance at him.

"She never completely recovered," he said. "I always suspected that, in some little corner of herself that couldn't be convinced by life, she hoped he would come back. You see, she had given up so much for him. Her family, all her friends, her society... She couldn't believe it was all for nothing."

"Not for nothing," I interjected. "She had you."

"Yes," he said. "And she was very devoted to me. Her eyes would light up every time I came into a room. She spent a lot of time with me. She shared as much of herself as she reasonably could with a young son. Perhaps with good reason. She was all I had."

"What about friends?" I asked.

"She had one close friend, a woman who had known her since childhood. They remained close until my mother—until she died."

"No, I meant you," I corrected him. "Did you have friends of your own?"

He looked at me. The ghost of a smile told me he knew what I was asking.

"Oh, yes, I had my friends. Not a lot. A couple of them were close," he said, giving me a brief private glance. "I wasn't completely isolated."

I blushed despite myself. I wondered who was more on the spot, Jordan or me. I had my own reasons for knowing that he had never outgrown our friendship. But even as I went along with his pretense that we didn't know each other, I felt my heart go out to him. My past with Jordan was a cornerstone of my life.

I had to make an effort to continue in my calm journalistic voice.

"I understand that your mother died when you were—thirteen, was it?" I asked.

"Yes. She died right after I went away to prep school," he said. "Heart failure. Her doctor hadn't suspected it."

I nodded in silence at his lie. I saw no reason to challenge it.

He looked at Christine. "And that school was where I met Christine's brother. It's ironic, isn't it? Just as my own past was being taken away, the future was already sending its signals.''

"Yes, it is.''

He was holding her hand, but in his eyes was once again that strange sidelong light, taking me in, admiring me perhaps, influencing me certainly in his favor. I glanced at the picture of his father. I wondered if Brady Sr. had had this subtle charm, or whether it belonged to Jordan alone.

"When I first met Christine she hated me,'' he said.

"That's a lie,'' Christine said, rumpling his hair affectionately. "I had an enormous crush on him, even though I was just a little girl.''

"Of course, I had to wait a long time for her to grow up,'' he said.

"Don't you dare say you're still waiting!'' Christine warned him with a laugh.

My eyes darted to her face in that instant, and my hand froze around my pen. I thought Jordan's choice of words was significant. At the same time Christine's playful, teasing gesture of rumpling his hair had made me see her in a different light.

"What kind of girl were you in those days?" I asked her.

"I was a tomboy," she said. "Always into mischief. Cuts and bruises everywhere, and friends' mothers calling my mother to tell her to get a better grip on me."

Every word she said struck a chord within me, and I knew Jordan was listening. I decided to add one more stroke to the picture.

"Were you a leader among your friends, or a follower?" I asked.

"Oh, a leader, definitely." She laughed. "I was terribly bossy. No one could tell me what to do."

Now I understood. She was the image of Lily. Not the Lily of today, but Lily as a girl, resurrected from a past known only to Jordan—and to me. Christine was Lily, modeled out of a foreign flesh, and out of memory.

Now I knew more than I had bargained for. And in Jordan's eyes I could see he knew I knew.

I turned the conversation to the early years of Jordan's business career. A few minutes later Christine excused herself, saying she had an appointment. I shook her hand and told her I hoped to be able to interview them together again.

"That would be nice." She smiled. Then, more confidentially, she said, "Don't let him take advantage of you. He can be a great liar when he wants."

Her words were still echoing in my ear when I sat down alone with Jordan.

"She's very attractive," I said. "And very charming. So natural and unaffected. I like her."

"So do I." Something in these words sounded significant, but I decided not to try to understand it completely.

"Perhaps we'd better stop for today," I said. "We've covered some painful subjects. You must be tired."

Jordan was looking at me. "I'm glad they sent you," he said. "Nothing happens by accident. I learned that a long time ago." The look in his eyes put me off balance.

"Jordan…"

He ran a hand through the hair that Christine had rumpled. The hair that Lily had rumpled when she was a girl.

"I've never stopped thinking about it," he said. "About that night…"

"Well, that's understandable," I said, my voice shaking a bit.

"I should have called you," he said. "Afterward. I couldn't get up my courage. I knew you had your own life. That night seemed so strange, somehow. Like a night stolen out of the world. Like Cinderella… You can't fit a night like that into real life."

"You're right," I reassured him hastily. "I felt the same way." After all, he was repeating the same logic that had kept me from getting in touch with him after our rendezvous. We saw eye to eye.

I thought suddenly of the night of the ball, now so long ago, when we were children poised on the threshold of real life. That night, too, had seemed stolen from life, a transgression.

Astonishingly, Jordan read my mind. "Like the night of the ball," he said. "Before my mother died. Something too good to be true. If you tried to hang on to it, it would wither like a flower.''

I nodded, shaken.

''But it wasn't left behind, was it?'' he asked. ''Because of you and me. Because of us.''

I felt cornered. Jordan was wielding the entire past like a weapon against which my emotions had no defenses.

''Your fiancée,'' I said deliberately. ''She reminds me of Lily.''

He was silent.

I hesitated an instant before asking, ''Is that what attracted you?''

He was looking at me through changed eyes. ''You know what attracted me.''

I looked down at my notes. ''Well,'' I said weakly. ''Enough about the past.''

''Isn't this interview about the past?'' he asked.

''And the future,'' I corrected him rather clumsily.

He merely looked at me as though I had put his own thought into words.

''I have to go,'' I said, gathering my things together.

Jordan was smiling at me. "You'll come back, though."

"Yes. I have a job to do." I stood up, struggling against the weakness in my legs.

He was on his feet, looking very confident, as though my attempts to see through him had only strengthened his hand.

"I'm glad fate brought you back to me again," he said. "I always hoped you'd come back. New York is a small town, in its way. I hoped we'd meet."

I picked up my briefcase. "I'm really going to have to go."

He saw me to the elevator. I went to my car on unsteady legs. I had a terrible feeling of history repeating itself. In his pretty young fiancée I had seen Lily, as hauntingly as one sees the features of a parent in a child who has been passed off as someone else's. The obsession in Jordan's eyes belied his polished exterior. He seemed literally possessed by the past. And when I mentioned Lily's name to him, I knew I had struck a nerve.

But in leaving Jordan I had not put my own emotional upheaval behind me. The deeper reason for my distress was waiting for me at home.

When I got there it was only three-thirty. Sarah was surprised to see me so soon.

"What happened?" she asked. "They didn't cancel, did they?"

"No," I said. "Just had to cut it short for today. You know how these rich folks are. We have to be at their beck and call."

"Well, that's how it works, I guess," she said.

"Where's my heartthrob?" I asked.

"Avoiding his nap," she said. "You'll see."

I went into my son's room and found him playing on the floor. He was drawing a series of circles, each one inside the other, with different-colored crayons on a large pad. He had an odd, composite look on his face, halfway between dreamy fascination and intent concentration, that made my heart go out to him.

"Hello, handsome," I said.

He got up to hug me. "Mama." The little

hands went around my neck, and I felt the moistness of his lips on mine.

"Have you had a nice day?" I asked.

"We went to the store," he said. "Sarah bought lots of cereal."

Sarah had children of her own, and often did some of her shopping with the boy. I had met her children—well-behaved little girls who took to my son—and had once helped her with a birthday party for the older one, Josie.

"What about you?" I asked. "Didn't you buy anything?"

"I don't buy things, silly," he said. "She gave me Life Savers."

I looked down at the pad. "Is that why you're drawing circles?" I asked.

He looked at the pad. "No." Then he cocked his head. "These aren't candy circles. Besides, each one is bigger."

I smiled at his sharp little intellect. "What a smart boy you are," I said. "Are you sure you're not tired?"

"I don't want my nap today."

"Well, why don't we go out to the park then?" I suggested.

He brightened immediately. The park at the end of our block was his favorite place. His little preschool friends came there with their mothers, and there was a whirligig that he never tired of riding on.

For some reason I wanted to be outdoors with him—and alone. I needed to test the reality of my situation with him, to make sure our happiness was real. The interview with Jordan seemed to have shaken my belief in it.

I helped him put his little jacket on, and took him down the street.

He pointed at a police car that was stopped by one of the row houses, its lights flashing silently while the officers were nowhere to be seen. One of the mothers from the block, who I knew slightly, was pointing it out to her little girl.

"I'd like to be a policeman when I grow up," my son said.

"Good for you." I smiled. "That's an important job. Will you give me a ride in your police car?"

"Mmm-hmm." He was still entranced by the flashing blue and white lights.

"Will you blow your siren while we take our ride?" I asked.

"I guess so," he said. "It's kind of loud."

"No siren, then. We don't want to disturb the neighbors. But will you flash the lights?"

"Yes."

We reached the park. I saw a couple of his friends huddling under the jungle gym, but I didn't want him to leave me yet.

"Will you stay with me for a minute?" I asked.

"Sure thing." He was imitating my own expression of reassurance. He was a sweet, tactful boy, alert to my feelings and eager to support me when he suspected I was feeling low.

There was a silence as we watched leaves turn this way and that in the trees. Someone opened a window across the park and leaned out. A well-dressed older man with a dog came down the block, pooper-scooper in hand. The sun seemed unable to make up its mind whether to light up the park or hide behind the clouds.

"Mom," he said.

"Yes, sweetie?"

"How many days is it until our vacation?"

We were going on a trip to the Adirondacks in the summer. It would be his first time camping, and he was excited about it.

"Let me see," I said. "This is May, and we're going in the first week of July. June has thirty days, so it must be about forty days until we go."

"Forty days." He was watching the man with the dog.

"A long time to wait," I said. "But it will pass. You'll see."

"Will we ever have a dog?" he asked.

"We might."

His little legs were swinging under the bench. His hand remained in mine. I never tired of the small warmth of him.

"Could our dog go camping, too?" he asked.

"If we had one, you mean."

"Yes."

"Sure he could. Lots of people take pets

camping. But he'd have to be careful not to bark and disturb the other campers.''

"He wouldn't bark," the boy said.

He was an imaginative child, always drawing pictures of fantastic situations and creatures. He liked to make up stories and tell them to me when I came to kiss him good-night. Often, as I told him a well-known bedtime story, like the cow that jumped over the moon, he would interrupt me with questions, embellishments, theories.

His brightness, his intelligence were always in the service of his tact. He wanted to make other people happy. He tried to soothe hurt in others, to heal conflict among his little friends. I had a mother's wishes for him, of course. Success, happiness, love. But I also saw the capacity for moral leadership in him, for reconciling, for bringing people together. It was fun to admire him as well as to love him. I considered myself the luckiest woman alive.

"Will you push me on the merry-go-round?" he asked.

"I'd be delighted," I said. "Let me just

sit another minute, though, and enjoy this quiet.''

He was silent, his fingers moving over mine as though over an abacus. I wondered whether he was trying to count up to forty.

The sun came out all at once. A shadow fell over his body and I turned to see a man standing there. His face was invisible, silhouetted against the sky. But his voice made my fingers go cold.

''I'd be happy to push you.''

It was Jordan. The boy turned to look at him. I had told him so often not to talk to strangers that caution kept him from answering.

''If your mom will let me,'' Jordan said.

My son turned to me. Still he said nothing.

''It's all right, sweetie,'' I said. ''This man is a friend of mine. His name is Mr. Brady.''

Jordan held out his hand. ''I'm very pleased to meet you.''

My heart missed a beat as I watched their hands touch. Dark eyes met dark eyes, small fingers disappeared into larger ones shaped the same, and the fervent sun made a mirror of the small face to the larger one. I felt faint. The whole world was calling to similar things to meet, to come closer to each other.

I looked into Jordan's eyes. I could see he knew everything. His face expressed reproach, but also sympathy, that infinite sympathy which was the secret of his charm, and which had found its way into my boy also.

I got up and went with them to the merry-go-round. Two of my son's little girlfriends rushed over. They all piled on, and Jordan and I began to push them. Two little girls and a boy, whirling counterclockwise, as Jordan and Lily and I had once whirled.

Counterclockwise. The expression seemed all too appropriate, for time itself was running backward as though that were its natural direction, into the past.

I still felt unsteady, but I took courage from the smile on my son's face. And Jordan's shadow, darkening the ground before me, seemed to offer me a precious balance.

"I just missed you at your apartment,"

Jordan said. "But I met your nanny. She said you were at the park with your son." He spoke the last word significantly.

I nodded. I told myself I should have expected this. If Jordan had failed to keep his secrets from me, why should I have expected to keep mine from him?

"What is his name?" Jordan asked in a murmur.

I shook my head. He knew so much now—how could he not know this last answer?

"Can't you guess?"

He touched my shoulder. "I've done enough guessing."

I turned to meet his eyes. Mine were full of tears.

"Jordan," I said.

8

My son's name was Nicholas, as a matter of fact. But I had dared to give him Jordan's name as a middle name and sometimes gave in to the temptation of using it when we were alone together.

Jordan came home to dinner with us that night. Nick took to him instantly. As for Jordan, he looked at my son through eyes in which amazement mingled with exultation. It was clear to see that he saw Nick as a miracle in flesh and blood.

Of course he knew the truth. That had been obvious even in the park. In all my life I have never seen anything so eloquent as the mirroring attraction of those two faces, the face of the man I loved and of the son I had stolen from him.

But Jordan said nothing about this. He

merely talked to the boy, played with him on my braided rug—and, every so often, looked up at me with an expression that melted my heart.

It was done. It was too late to wish that it had never happened. The two realities I had thought permanently separate were now mingled. I could only stand and watch now.

We made love that night, after the boy was asleep. In Jordan's passion, which was slow and tender, I felt his memory of what had happened to us together four years ago. My own response took me back to that night, and to the strange complicity of the world and of time in this coupling.

But it was more complicated now, for in his embrace I felt his deepening, consuming love for his son. I was not alone in his arms. I could not flatter myself that it was for me alone that he was here. No more than I flattered myself, the night of our rendezvous, that it was I alone whom Jordan had come to find.

None of this had to do with me alone. No, I was part of something bigger, something mingled and composite that occupied a central place in Jordan's heart. And my son had become a key part of that larger structure.

Jordan looked at the sleeping boy before he left that night. At the boy, and back at me. Then he left, possibly not dreaming what a shambles he had made of my carefully controlled life.

My profile interview with him continued. Day after day I met with him during his free hours. I attended some of his meetings with business associates. Sometimes we had dinner together. Jordan was very busy, but he always found time for me.

A few times Christine was present at our meetings. He was as affectionate toward her as ever. They joked about their relationship, they acted like lovers. He held her hand as he looked at me. But I knew he had held me in his arms the night before. And he had held my son to his breast, drinking him in, regretting the four years he had not known him, measuring the miracle of knowing him now.

Once, embarrassingly, I interviewed

Christine alone. I asked her about her professional ambitions, her plans for starting a family with Jordan. She seemed a shade cooler without him there, but I was sure she suspected nothing.

As the weeks went by I began to sense impatience in her. My concentration on Jordan's past life seemed to make her nervous. She wanted the interview to be over. I could feel her desire to get married. She was tired of this lengthy preamble to her future. She wanted to be Jordan's wife, to abolish his past.

I let it go on. I felt like a criminal, but I could not help myself. I was paralyzed. And I could not help feeling that Jordan himself was in the grip of something outside himself. In his caresses there seemed too much passion to be bestowed on one woman. He was making love to a dream. He would look at me as I lay waiting for him in my bed, and his eyes had a haunted expression that made me feel at once wanted and alone. His embrace warmed me beautifully, and yet he seemed a million miles away, somehow. Because of this, our trysts were always painful, sometimes beyond ecstasy. It was like falling down a hole into another world.

Jordan and the boy had hit it off from the beginning. Nick was, despite all my efforts, starved for adult male companionship. Jordan quickly became his friend, taught him things I couldn't, showed him ways of feeling that only a man knows, that no woman can imitate.

Soon Nick wanted Jordan to say goodnight to him. He wanted to speak to Jordan when Jordan telephoned. He wanted to show Jordan his books and toys and drawings. Their affection grew quickly. They were making up for lost time after having been unfairly separated for four long years.

I felt an impulse to protest against what was happening. But it seemed too late to stop any of it. It had its own momentum, a surge that came from deep in the past and could not be denied.

One day in June Jordan ushered me into his office and told me his engagement to Christine was broken off.

"It was long overdue," he said. "We

weren't right for each other. She knew it, too. She seemed more relieved than anything else.''

I was not so much surprised by this news as defeated. I had felt it coming, somewhere in our interviews, in his manner and in that of Christine, but I had told myself this was a false perception based on my own mingled feelings, all of which were out of control.

"Jordan," I said. "I don't know what to say. If I had never come along..."

"If you had never come along I would never have known a moment's happiness," he said.

"You're exaggerating," I began to protest.

"Kate, I want to live with you," he interrupted. "And with my son."

I responded to this with an anger that surprised me.

"Did Christine figure out the truth?" I asked.

"About us?"

I shook my head.

"Did she figure out how you were using her?"

"Using her? What do you mean?" He seemed surprised. I realized he didn't see the truth himself.

I didn't have the heart to attack him, but I had to say something in protest.

"Jordan, this isn't me," I said.

"What do you mean?"

"This isn't me you've found."

He looked at me. He brushed a strand of my hair from my eyes. He looked hurt.

"What are you talking about?"

I took a deep breath, fighting for the courage to confront him. "It wasn't me you were looking for all this time, all these years," I said. "I know that. I tried to tell myself it didn't matter. But it does matter. Everything matters—between a man and a woman."

"Aren't you being a little presumptuous?" he asked. "Telling me what I've been looking for all my life?"

"I can see it in your eyes, every time you look at me," I said. "I'm just the—the connection. I'm your link to it all. To the past, to Lily... And because of Nick, the past is real enough for you to grab on to. But none of it is really me. It's all a dream.'' I looked away, avoiding his eyes. ''It's just as you said in our interview. Some nights can't be fitted into the real world. They should be left alone. But you and I—we're not leaving it alone.''

Then I turned back to him. To my surprise I saw that my words, which had cost me so much, had had no effect on him.

''I won't ask anything of you,'' he said. ''I realize I have no claim on you. You're a free woman. Nick is your son. His future and yours—it's all your own decision. I don't flatter myself that I have rights in the matter.'' He looked up at me softly. ''Is there anyone else? A man?''

A sound somewhere between a laugh and a sob escaped my lips.

''No. There is no other man.'' These words hurt more than anything that had gone before.

''But there was, once,'' he said. ''You lived with a man for a long time.''

"How did you know about that?" I asked.

He shrugged. "I was curious. It's common knowledge, anyway."

I shook my head, smiling. "That was nothing, Jordan."

Jordan's relief was obvious. "I'm not asking you to commit yourself, or your son, in any way," he said. "But please give me this chance for happiness. Do it out of the kindness of your heart. You can't know how warm, how alive I feel when I'm with you. I've never felt that way, not since my mother died, perhaps not even before that. Let me share what I can of Nick. Please, Kate."

For an instant I felt physically weak. I hung my head before him, almost like a guilty child. I knew what must be done, but I couldn't do it. I had exhausted my store of courage.

"There are punishments for things like this," I said. "Aren't there?"

He put his arms around me. "Haven't we both been punished enough already?"

I said nothing. I understood what he

meant. But I also saw the other side of the coin. Life had not been easy for me, but in some ways I had been lucky. Now he was asking me to risk the small world I had built for myself.

"How can love be wrong?" he asked. "Besides, I would risk anything to be with you."

He might as well be saying, *with the two of you.* I knew that never in this world would he say, in his heart, *with you. With Kate.*

Nevertheless I gave up.

"All right," I said.

9

Jordan moved some of his things to my little place on Staten Island and commuted to work with me. We both hurried home to be with Nick. Sometimes we took the ferry together, but often Jordan got there before I did, and was playing with the boy while Sarah watched when I got home.

We were a strange threesome. Nick was the child of a single parent. Jordan was an orphan—as I was. We had been brought together, the three of us, by a colossal accident—and by a dream. Yet, amazingly, we had the same biological claim to be a family as anyone else did. Only the marriage certificate was lacking to authenticate us as part of the real world.

I allowed myself to fall gently into this irony, into this unlikely fate. And it was a

good feeling. All my life I had been standing firmly on my own two feet. Falling was
a part of life I had missed. I savored it hun-
grily, unscrupulously.

Before Nick started school in the fall Jordan found us a new apartment, on Central
Park West. It was large and quiet, in a
building which had children Nick could
play with. We went to the park every day.
Often Jordan met us there. I watched as he
walked among the autumn trees, holding his
son's hand. They were similar, physically.
Nick was slim and dark, as Jordan had been
when we were children with Lily. When he
grew up he would probably be tall, as Jordan was now. I coveted this thought like a
secret pride.

Often I came home from work to find
Jordan already there with Nick. "Look
who's here," he would say when I arrived,
pointing to me as Nick looked up from his
toys. Somehow I remember them as always
being on the floor together, either in the living room or in Nick's bedroom. Jordan was
either watching the boy color a picture, or
helping him build something, or staging

elaborate dramas involving Nick's collection of little knights and ladies and cowboys and soldiers. A wildly heterogeneous collection of characters, all joining in one epic saga in which there was always a king, a lady and, of course, a Bad Guy.

"Come and join us," Jordan would urge me. "The game is just getting good." Then, to the boy, "We can't really finish it right unless she helps us, can we?"

Nick shook his head, amused.

It was that way. To a casual observer it might have seemed that Jordan was enjoying a second childhood through my son. But this was not true. Jordan was simply trying to get close to Nick as fast as possible, and to give him as much as he could. If childhood means accepting what is given without wondering whether it will be taken away, there was nothing childish about what Jordan was doing. The shadow of his own losses was in every look he lavished on his son.

"Which one is she going to choose?" he would ask, looking at the tiny lady. "The Black Knight or the White Knight?" Or

again, "Are they going to run away together? Or will there be a war?" He always
left the decisions up to Nick, and he seemed
to covet them, once made, as though they
were precious artifacts of the boy's growing
personality.

He made a great show of admiring me.
"Your mother is looking very pretty today,
isn't she?" he would ask, invoking Nick's
judgment.

And Nick, smiling, would look away and
nod as I blushed despite myself at the compliment.

"I wish she would stay home more often," Jordan added seriously. "She works
too much. Don't you think?"

To this the boy always agreed. He didn't
like it when I went off to an interview, or
when I closeted myself in my little office to
work at my computer.

Sometimes I would hear Jordan talking
to Nick about me when I was out of the
room.

"Do you think she's mad at me?" he
would ask. "Or is she just tired?"

Or again, "This morning she looked at

me in the funniest way. I couldn't tell whether she was worried about something or whether she was just thoughtful.'' Jordan behaved as though Nick knew me better than he himself did.

Always the boy would reassure him, saying, ''She's fine,'' ''She's not mad at you,'' or words to that effect. These little exchanges amused me and unnerved me at the same time, because I sensed in Jordan's professed uncertainty about me a genuine worry that he didn't feel sure about my feelings. And indeed, I had never felt free to let him see all those feelings.

As for Jordan himself, he talked easily and volubly about our new life and what it meant to him.

''I always suspected that I would never have a son,'' he told me once. ''I don't know why, but that idea was always in me. I suppose it had something to do with my childhood. I just thought I wasn't going to be lucky that way.''

And he hugged me, as though to thank me. I said nothing. I was silenced by the contrast between his emotions, which

seemed so simple, and my own, which were
so complicated.

On a brisk fall afternoon Jordan would
breeze in from work and announce, "Now,
there are several things we could do this
afternoon. We could go to the park. We
could go to the movies. We could take a
ride." Then, to Nick, "I can't decide. I'm
of three minds. What about you? How
many minds do you have?"

More often than not, if Nick himself was
torn between two plans, Jordan would announce, "The solution is simple. We'll do
both." This often resulted in outings which
bordered on the grueling, but Nick never
seemed to mind.

The old routine of my life alone with my
son was gone now. Jordan brought excitement in the door with him. When he wasn't
leading us on an outing, he was drinking
Nick in. He saved finger paintings, crayon
drawings, first messages written in penciled
capital letters, with passionate absorption.
He took thousands of snapshots. Cursing his
little flash camera which failed to capture
the natural light as it fell on Nick's face, he

bought a Pentax and took a course in photography.

This bath of love could hardly fail to overflow onto me. I began to feel myself part of a real family. I stopped thinking of our distant past together, Jordan's and mine, as a guilty thing which cast a shadow over our life with Nick. Instead I had a peculiar, restful sense of a circle closing, of three becoming as one, just as I had once felt as a girl, when the partners were Jordan and Lily and me.

I remembered my book about the little girl with her magic hourglass. It seemed that the return of Jordan to my life, and its creation of a new life to make us three, was part of a mystical turn of my own hourglass, which reversed historical time in order to re-create a special moment using new flesh, new events. But this reversal was not a result of mere chance. It was ruled by a strange passion, the passion of the number three.

That winter Jordan bought a house in Rye, a relatively short train ride from the city, and we decorated it together. Then we began to spend weekends there. This gave us opportunities for fresh air, for silence and for long drives, which were impossible in the city.

It was a small house, with two bedrooms, a living room and a little den at the back where we watched TV. Jordan seemed to want it small. I sometimes caught a look of serene contentment on his face as we huddled together in the kitchen for breakfast, or watched a show with Nick in the den, with windows that looked out on a tiny backyard and alley. I think Jordan wanted the house to embrace us, to pull us close. No doubt his memories of the inhuman sprawl of Brookfield, with his frightened mother hiding in her bedroom, had something to do with this.

When I look back on those times I remember the excitement of Jordan's constant plans, the sense that something was always happening or about to happen. But I also see images of peace and languor. Jordan pointing to his easy chair, in which Nick had fallen asleep, and smiling at me with amused pride. Jordan singing the boy to sleep, the murmur of his voice reaching me easily in the next room. The three of us sitting on the couch watching a TV show or perhaps a rented movie, eating popcorn they had made together according to Nick's recipe, with paprika and Parmesan cheese.

If I seem slow to mention my private relationship with Jordan, our intimacy, our lovemaking, it is because these things were somehow inseparable from our delight in the boy and in our life as a family. When Jordan came to me in the night, his caresses full of tenderness and yearning, I still felt the smiles he had lavished on Nick and me all day. His very possession of me seemed a celebration of what we had created together. I learned to match my own ecstasy to this particular color of love, to make myself his partner in this special way.

I never once entertained the idea of demanding a greater commitment from Jordan. Had I not, after all, stolen this child from him one moonlit night when he was in an exalted mood, at an improbable rendezvous, and thinking of the past far more than he was thinking of me? Had I not kept the boy for four years before chance allowed Jordan to learn of his existence? I had no claims on him.

I was my own brake, my own strict and inflexible limit in this. I had heard the name Lily on Jordan's lips before I heard my own. I had seen the light of his affection on Christine's face before I saw it turned to me. And when that affection did turn to me it was always through Nick. I did not flatter myself that I was the woman Jordan loved. My job was to be satisfied with what I had. Asking for more—the slightest bit more—might bring disaster.

As an orphan, I had had a long life of learning to limit my expectations, of learning to make do with what I had. I told myself that in making no claims on Jordan I was facilitating his happiness with Nick. I was a modern woman, after all. I was grown-up. I knew how to give love, and to enjoy closeness, without imposing unrealistic conditions.

But I did make one "mental error," as the athletes call it so eloquently. I dared to congratulate myself on all this, and to think of myself as a woman in control of her life, a woman who had come to terms with the world, making prudent sacrifices at the proper times and then being rewarded for them.

It was not that simple.

In the spring Jordan had to go on a ten-day business trip to Europe, so I called Lily and asked her whether Nick and I could come back home for a visit. She was delighted. Her little daughters, Susie and Beth, adored Nick, and Rob looked upon him affectionately as the son he had never had.

I had not told Lily who Nick's father was. I think she assumed it was Brett. I presented myself as a single parent whose love life I did not feel like discussing. Lily accepted that.

I sometimes wondered if Lily saw Jordan in Nick's face or manner. She never mentioned Jordan's name, had never mentioned it since the night before her wedding. And I, of course, was not about to bring it up. This was my one secret from her.

We drove up on a Sunday, Nick with a

small bag of books and me with my computer. It was a good time from the beginning. Rob welcomed Nick with open arms, showed him around his workshop, and during our visit helped him put together a model car he had bought for the occasion.

Their life was more suburban now. Rob belonged to the country club, and he had managed to convince Lily to play golf with him. She was not a good player, and she made fun of the country club wives behind their backs, but she went along with Rob. She belonged to the PTA, she did charity work in the community and she had an active social life. But her family remained her real interest and vocation.

Rob was, ironically, growing to resemble his father more. Not in his body, which remained tall and slender, but in his impatience, his worry about money and in a certain stubbornness which would come over him at times. He was sure to inherit the family business as well as his father's considerable wealth, and I suspected that this legacy was weighing on him psychologically. He complained about the people he had to do business with. He said they were sharks, trying to steal from him. He worked longer hours, saying he couldn't trust anyone else to get anything done right. He seemed to have difficulty coping with leisure time. He closeted himself in his office upstairs and worked even when he was home.

His old political liberalism had been eaten away, gradually, by his struggles with business problems. He complained bitterly about big government, about red tape and taxes. Once in a while he would decry those who lived off the country without contributing anything to it, and Lily would roll her eyes to me. I dared to argue with him about it, especially when he criticized labor unions and health benefits for the aged. Lily took my side, amused, and even told him to his face, ''Rob, you're getting more like your father every day. If you don't watch out, you're going to wake up one morning with a cigar in your mouth.''

Sometimes his stubbornness bordered on the infantile. He would dig his heels in over some small thing like which friend to invite to dinner, which piano teacher for the girls to go to or even which dress Lily should wear to a party. A dozen times I saw Lily give in patiently. At other times she would lash out at him, "Why don't you just relax for once? It's not as though the world were going to come to an end!"

I now realized that the episode of Rob's infidelity had left a mark on their marriage. Rob's devotion to Lily seemed a bit more strained now, a bit less spontaneous. I occasionally felt silences between them that made me turn my eyes away.

But sometimes he seemed like the Rob of old, relaxed and affectionate and even boyish. He would cross a room impulsively to hug Lily, and she would speak to him in little endearments. He brought flowers home to her almost as a matter of routine. Sometimes when he was embracing her, the girls would rush into the room and demand to be included in what now became a family hug, two adults and two children laughing as they bounced against each other.

At these moments I felt that, though the old alliance between Lily and Rob might have been attenuated by time, their marriage had survived its worst years, and would endure. Because of the children, perhaps, but also because of something unspoken between Lily and Rob that was too subtle for an outsider like me to measure.

The girls, Susie and Beth, were both very pretty. Beth took after Rob more, but they both looked like miniature versions of Lily—tall, skinny, bright-eyed, full of energy. They doted on Nick, and renewed an assortment of games they had played with him on our last visit. They looked upon him as a cousin, and since they had no brother, found him exotic and exciting. Their playfulness, sometimes reckless, was balanced by his natural tact and gentleness. They made a lovely trio.

As for Lily, she seemed to covet Nick as delightedly as her daughters did. She would take him on her knee when the girls weren't running around with him outside, and talk to him about his own interests. I could see she missed having a son. And, with considerable pride, I noticed how impressed she was by Nick's unusual imagination and sweetness.

"He's such a gentleman," she told me our third evening there. "Watch out, Kate. Kids grow up fast. These two may be contending for his hand in marriage before you know it."

I laughed. The idea seemed crazy. I was not in the habit of looking ahead the way Lily did. I lived in the moment. But of course her girls were older, and she lived in the real world. She saw contingencies, eventualities, that I did not.

"Which one do you think he would choose?" I asked.

"Hmm," she mused. "Beth is quieter, more like you. Though she can be a hellion when her sister eggs her on. He might pick her, because she's more like his mother. On the other hand, Susie has so much flash. She's not afraid of anything. If she were to set her cap for him, I don't know if he would be able to resist."

We watched them play, and I pondered these assessments. The three children reminded me of us as children. In those days

Lily had been the daring, willful one; I the more reflective and diffident; and Jordan the peacemaker, the diplomat.

"I'm not sure he would be completely happy with either of them," she said. "He's going to need a very special girl when the time comes. These two might not be good enough for him."

"Nonsense." I laughed. "They'll be good enough for anyone. Look how lovely they are."

One night I insisted on baby-sitting the three children while Lily and Rob went to a dinner party being given by some friends of theirs. They protested that they wanted to show me off to their friends—they were proud of my career and wanted to tell people about it—but I wouldn't listen.

The girls and I made macaroni and cheese and a huge pizza. I ate a slice of the pizza with some salad while the children devoured all the rest with an alacrity that astonished me. The two girls were voracious eaters despite their skinny bodies.

After dinner I sat on the porch going

through some notes for an article while the kids played on the lawn. I saw them chase a firefly from bush to bush, their cries echoing in the stillness of the evening. I felt an odd intimacy with them, as though my own lost self was charging around the lawn along with them. The distinction between reality and fantasy floated tiredly in the night air, and I let myself go to thoughts of my life with Lily so long ago, when no adult problems could trouble us, when only the vivid sense of discovery and adventure united us.

Later, when I put them all to bed in Beth's room, where they were to sleep on the floor in sleeping bags, I remembered the times Lily and I slept over at Jordan's house. His mother would let us take our pick among the countless unused guest rooms, and her servants would clean and air the space before we used it. The room would be as unfamiliar to Jordan as to us when we settled down to sleep.

As I kissed the children good-night I allowed myself the brief fantasy that I was the mother of all three. But in that instant my inner clock took a brusque turn backward, and I felt as though it was Lily and Jordan and my own childhood self I was mothering with my kiss.

After the children were asleep I felt restless. I was too tired to concentrate on my work, but too jittery to watch a TV show or to read. I paced the house, looking at books and knickknacks and family photos that had now become familiar to me.

I ended up somehow in Lily's studio upstairs. After a hiatus of several years, she had taken up painting again. There were watercolors pinned to planks on the walls. A couple of pieces of sculpture, long neglected, stood on drop cloths. The place smelled of dust, paint and varnish.

I had never been up here alone. It was Lily's only refuge from the family. The girls were forbidden admittance here, and Rob himself never entered it. He felt his wife needed an inner sanctum.

In the corner I noticed the old hope chest that Lily had had as a girl. I remembered that there were items there concerning me and our old days together. I knelt down before it and looked at the lock.

It was a brass combination lock, with three little rollers. Many years ago, I recalled, Lily had told me the combination and even made me memorize it. I could still hear her voice—*We'll never have secrets from each other.*

I recalled the promise, but not the combination. I smiled to think that in this small, irrelevant way I was unfaithful to our girlish past.

And yet, when I fingered the rollers idly, I seemed to feel something in my hand, a sort of response. I held my breath, let my fingers roll the first three numbers they liked—and suddenly the lock came open. My fingers, clever with the wisdom of the past, had remembered the combination when my mind had long since forgotten it.

I opened the trunk. Inside I found some objects that reminded me of my own trunk, retrieved at Aunt Clara's after her death. There were books, girls' jewelry, skates, a couple of dolls. Underneath them I noticed a fold of familiar-looking fabric. I unearthed it cautiously. I caught my breath as I realized what it was. It was the dress Lily had worn to the ball the night we made our promise.

I pulled out the dress and looked at it. The garment had the patina of age about it, and the satin was discolored and faded. But it was the dress I had made so lovingly. It had a sad eloquence in its very antiquity. I could almost feel Lily's firm adolescent body fitting into it, and hear her nervous protests about going to the dance without me.

So Lily had not forgotten. A creature of present and future time, she had kept enough of the past in her to hang on to the dress. It was like a flower pressed in a book, a reminder of our "threeness," and the last and greatest night of our youth together.

I wondered what Rob would think if he ever found this. I guessed that Lily would laugh about it. But I also suspected that she would never show it to him of her own accord.

At the bottom of the chest, beneath the folded dress, was a scrapbook. I pulled it out and opened it. I was in search of pictures of us as children.

I found them. Tiny snapshots taken by Mr. France with his Brownie, others taken by Carl in his photography years, a couple of class pictures from school. I also found two pictures, taken I knew not by whom, which showed us girls with Jordan at Brookfield. How small we were! How foreign to the two grown women who were together now. I was touched by Lily's nostalgia, her fidelity to the past. She had kept these pictures.

I turned the page. I saw the same picture of Lily and Jordan at the ball that I had found in my own trunk at Clara's. Alongside it was a picture of Jordan with his mother. I realized they must have both been taken by a circulating photographer.

Jordan's mother wore an artfully gay expression that veiled her desperation. She looked so young! Hardly older than I myself, now. But she had only a few days to live.

Jordan looked very innocent, very much a thirteen-year-old boy. The hourglass turned a bit inside me, and I could see his resemblance to Nick, as Nick would perhaps look a few years from now. Surely Nick would have that same handsome, slightly melancholy look, and that straight young body.

On the next page was a picture that surprised me. It showed Jordan at Groton. He was older, at least fourteen or fifteen. This was a Jordan I had never seen. I had been out of touch with him at the time, and since our adult relationship began I had not thought to ask him if he had any pictures from his prep school and college years. Those years were a blank for me.

I began to sense danger as I turned more pages. But I could not stop my hand. There were more pictures of Jordan, at college, with friends, and even as a young man, with some unidentified business associates. There were a few articles about his early successes in business.

I was just registering the fact that these pictures were too recent, and indicated too recent an interest in Jordan, when, to my amazement, I saw a picture of Nick. I pulled it out and turned it over. I saw Jordan's handwriting. *Nick, age 4 years 3 months.*

A letter, folded on itself, was alongside the picture. My fingers trembled as I opened it. The sight of Jordan's handwriting brought a sound from my throat, somewhere between a gasp and a sob.

Whenever I look at his face, I think of you, and of us…

I put my hands over my eyes, almost as people do in the movies when something on the screen is too frightening for them to look at. Then I folded the letter. My fingers were frozen despite the heat of the attic. My breath came short.

I opened my eyes to put the things back. But the letter was still open enough for me to see the last lines.

…won't ever forget. Promise, promise…

I love you,
Jordan

I put the letter back where I had found it. I turned a few more pages, but saw that they were blank. I realized they were reserved for future pictures.

I looked in the chest for other letters, but there were none. Apparently they were kept somewhere else. This one had likely been left in the scrapbook because it was the most recent.

I was shocked. The picture of Nick had been taken with Jordan's new Pentax, very recently. It was a picture taken from the new life I had with Jordan and Nick.

Jordan was in touch with Lily. He had perhaps never been out of touch with her. Or out of love with her.

Vainly I fought to recover my balance. Five minutes ago I had been congratulating myself complacently on my discovery of Lily's nostalgia for our youth together. Congratulating myself that I had found the grown-up Jordan, that I knew his body, had his son. Now I was confronted by a timeless truth that I had tried to lull myself into forgetting. It was Lily Jordan loved, all along.

For the first time I truly understood the

expression "My whole life flashed before my eyes." From the very beginning, our life with Jordan was in this scrapbook. But that life had not ended for Lily when Jordan went away. Lily and Jordan had not forgotten each other.

A cruel imp inside my mind pushed me quickly to a further conclusion. If Jordan and Lily had remained in touch, perhaps they had seen each other. Why not?

True, Lily was a stay-at-home, a wife and mother. And Jordan had roamed far afield in his life. But now the image of the old Brady house reared darkly before my mind's eye. A place that had been preserved stubbornly by Jordan, despite the fact that it was full of tragic memories. A shrine, certainly. An obsession. But also a possible meeting place.

This thought was so painful that I found my hands pressing on top of the hope chest as though to keep it closed. The truth hidden away here was too multiple to behold in a single instant. It was rooted in the whole past like an inoperable disease, an infection of the years. Not a single one of my memories, my beliefs, was free of the contagion of it.

"I should have known," I murmured to myself weakly. I felt like a fool. The more so because, in my time with Jordan, I had flattered myself that I was possessing something which had been out of reach for Lily. Now I realized I should have drawn the opposite conclusion. If Jordan found his way to me, he must have found his way back to her first.

I left the attic and went into the children's room. I looked at their faces, eager for some sign that the old reality I had taken for granted still existed. The girls were sleeping with their arms flung wide across the floor; Susie's hand was touching Nick's shoulder. I felt a crazy impulse to pluck him out of there, to take him away with me.

But where could I run to? Back to New York, to the arms of a man who, every time he held me, thought only of Lily? Who saw her face in his son every time he looked at him, just as I saw Jordan's face in the boy when I kissed him? Who saw her face behind mine the night we met at the Fertile

Crescent, when he lay down with me in the grass?

My imaginary hourglass came mockingly to my mind now. Its grains of sand, mingled in a thousand different ways, were not my grains alone. They were inextricably mixed with those of Lily and Jordan, and of their love. No corner of my life, no matter how remote, was free of it.

I went to my room to bed, deciding not to wait up for Lily and Rob. I was sure the look on my face would reveal to her that I knew everything. I needed the night to compose myself.

I did not sleep. But the next morning, when my son came quietly into my bedroom to wake me with a kiss, I was ready. I held him close for a long time, and then went downstairs with him, my face wearing the smile I had spent the whole night working on.

10

Every adult knows what it feels like to look back and pick out the happiest year of his or her life. It is a strange feeling, because one inevitably finds a considerable amount of adversity and even sadness surrounding the glowing memory of contentment. No one slips through this world without injury. Often our times of happiness turn out to be the times when we were the most flexible, when we asked the least of life.

My "happiest year" lasted much longer than a year. It began the day that Jordan followed Nick and me to our little park, and asked to move in with us. And, curiously enough, it did not end the night I found the scrapbook in Lily's attic.

I never told Jordan what I had found out. I decided I would gain little by accusing him of deceiving me, especially after my own deceptions over the years. Certainly I had a lot to lose. A family, in fact—or the closest thing to a normal family I was ever likely to see.

Besides, upon reflection I felt that what I had found did not really come as a surprise. It simply confirmed my intuition about the life we had been living—all of us.

So I made Jordan's secret my own secret. I didn't forget what I had learned in Lily's attic, nor did I try to deny it. I realized that sometimes a great love is not conceived among two people only. If I could accept the fact that my son loved Jordan as well as me, why could I not accept the fact that Jordan himself had never stopped loving Lily? Couldn't he love me, too?

And if, in some way, Jordan saw Lily in his son, because she had been so deeply embedded in his heart when the boy was conceived, could I not share this love with her?

I decided I could. In fact, the old me, the me of my childhood, came forward to help me in this. I had grown up believing in our "threeness" as the deepest wellspring of

my own love. Something of the exultation
I once felt in sewing Lily's beautiful dress
came to me now, and I threw myself into
this dream. I was willing to share Jordan
with Lily, because that brought Jordan back
to me. I felt the unseen circle of our existence closing sweetly around me, including
me and giving me a life.

I stopped believing in exclusivity. I became a patron of the multiple, the complex.
And I thought that by being so adaptable I
was insuring myself against unhappiness.

My strategy worked. Years passed, and
Jordan and I watched our son grow. By the
time Nick was eight years old, he had many
friends, both in the city and in Rye, and was
admired by his teachers for his politeness in
class, his humor and imagination. Jordan
had gone on to greater and greater things in
his career, while I had cut back my work
as a journalist so as to spend more time with
Nick. We were busy, happy people. Life
had given us the gift we wanted most, and
we were not inclined to second-guess our
happiness.

During the spring after Nick's eighth

birthday the routine of our lives underwent a change. Some golf-course scholars approached Jordan with the proposition of restoring the golf course his father had built so long ago in Summer Harbor. The architect of the course, now dead, was a legend, and he had mentioned the course prominently in his autobiography, expressing gratification that such players as Ben Hogan and Byron Nelson had called it one of the most original courses they had ever played.

Jordan approved their idea. And he went further. He decided to restore the sprawling home in which he had spent his childhood. It was no good as a house, of course, for it was so huge that no one could ever want to live in it. But its own architectural style was interesting, and it would make an ideal clubhouse for the restored golf course. It had been built so solidly by Brady Sr. that the engineers who looked at it assured Jordan that it could be restored. A lot of the old furnishings could play a part in the various salons and libraries, and use could be found for the countless bedrooms.

Jordan got excited about the idea. He told

me he saw it as a way of making peace,
indirectly, with the father who had abandoned him so long ago.

"I think it will be fitting," he said. "He
lost everything, but he wanted people to
know he had been here. There was that passion in him to leave a mark. I think it would
bring me a certain peace of mind to give
him his wish."

I was astonished by this generosity toward a man who had, as far as I could tell,
brought Jordan nothing but misery. I suspected there was something more here, a
way for Jordan to rehabilitate his sense of
his own past. I think he felt exiled in the
world, and he wanted to create for himself
an ancestral soil to which he could return.

I didn't go with him on any of the trips
to Maine. He said he wanted to surprise me
when the whole project was finished.

I couldn't help worrying about those
trips. Lily was in Summer Harbor. Perhaps
she was the magnet drawing Jordan back,
and the golf course only a pretext for him
to be near her. But I never said anything,

either to Jordan or to Lily, and I never tried to check up on him.

When the project was nearly completed, there was a lot of publicity about it, not only in golf magazines, but in national publications. "Magnate Restores Brookfield." That sort of thing. Jordan had picked a board of directors for the restored course, which was to be public. (A nod to his father's bitterness over not being admitted to the local course so long ago.) The clubhouse would be an architectural showcase.

Jordan suggested that Nick and I accompany him to Maine for the official opening. He asked me to call Lily and tell her we were coming. He wanted to meet her husband and daughters, he said. I made the call; Lily eagerly agreed.

Thus the silent wheel turned underneath us once more, and we strode heedlessly into the future as though it could never take us unawares again.

I looked forward with mixed feelings to the trip. Lily now knew that Jordan and I were living together—I could hardly hide that fact from her. But I had told her I met him through my profile on him in *The New Yorker*. I had never officially enlightened her as to Nick's paternity. I assumed Jordan had told her everything, but I had, of course, never asked Jordan about this. My own silence put me in a false position, but I could see no way out of it. The truth about our lives could not be spoken aloud. It announced itself in wordless, enormous ways, like the face of my son.

It turned out that my worries were unnecessary. Our arrival went smoothly. When we drove up to their house, Lily and Rob were waiting on the lawn, and the girls were with them, anxious to greet Nick.

Rob was happy to meet Jordan, whom he considered a celebrity from a business point of view. Lily threw her arms around Jordan, exclaiming how handsome he was and how well he had turned out. It was a brilliant act.

"Just look at you!" she said, rumpling his hair and beaming at Rob and me. "Oh, Jordan, I missed you all these years. How could I be so selfish as to lose touch?"

"Well, sometimes it isn't easy," Jordan offered tactfully.

"Rob, you've heard me talk about Jordan," she said. "When we were children we were thick as thieves. Kate, too. I lived for the three of us. They were my only world." She turned to me. "Tell him, Kate. Tell him how it was."

Embarrassed, I managed a smile. Meanwhile Nick had gone to Lily's side and was holding her hand.

"Hello, handsome," she said. "I'm so glad you could be here, too."

Nick looked from her to Jordan with something inquisitive in his eyes that pierced my heart. I couldn't help wondering whether he sensed the feeling between them.

A few moments later Lily and I were in the kitchen together. She hugged me close and said, "Sweetie, I'm so happy for you. And for Nick. He couldn't have a better daddy and mommy." She looked at me. "Seeing you here together, all three, is so wonderful for me."

That was all. I was amazed by her blitheness in congratulating me while tactfully hiding the truth that might have hurt or embarrassed me. As far as she was concerned, Jordan and Nick and I were a family, and there was nothing more to be said. I went along with her gratefully.

When we returned to the living room I saw that Jordan was watching Lily. I tried to see her through his eyes. Time had only increased her beauty by adding lines, contours of experience and pain that deepened her. She was thinner now, a bit pale, and this only made her seem more romantic, more feminine. It occurred to me that in a haunting way she had come to resemble her late mother. Like Mrs. France she was sprightly, full of good humor and ready for fun. But there was something faraway in her eyes, something complicated and sad that she did her best to conceal.

She was a beautiful woman, perhaps more so now than ever before. I could see that Jordan had difficulty keeping his eyes from returning to her as we talked. I couldn't help feeling jealous at this; yet I followed his gaze and admired her myself, as I had done when we were girls.

Jordan invited Rob to play the course with him the next day. When Rob said Lily was a golfer Jordan invited her, too, but she refused.

"You men go and play," she said. "I'm not going to spoil your beautiful new golf course with a bunch of topped balls and divots."

It was a remarkable visit in every way. The girls were all over Nick, showing him a hundred new possessions and games. Rob and Lily were perfect hosts, showering us with good wishes. There was an atmosphere of gentle harmony among us, tinged with a peculiar undercurrent of excitement.

Jordan expressed an interest in meeting Lily's family, and we took him over to the France house. The old place seemed to have the same attraction for Jordan that it had always had for me. But the France family had not found much happiness over the years. Christine had divorced her second husband and got in touch with Lily only when she wanted to borrow money. Old

Mr. France had died a couple of years ago, emptied of all interest in life by his wife's death. Eric, the prodigal younger brother, was seriously ill in California, and Lily was making regular trips out there to nurse him. She begged him to come home, but he still refused to see the family.

Carl, the older brother, had added a girl-friend to his life, a sweet local lady named Rina who had been his fiancée for several years. But he seemed to have no plan to marry her. He still lived upstairs in the bedroom of his youth, surrounded by his manuals and electronic equipment and inscrutable plans.

As for Ingrid, she was very much the dried-up spinster, though she was overweight and quite massive when she sat in a chair. She dominated all the obligatory France family gatherings, serving casseroles, roasts and pastries whose recipes remained her well-guarded secret. She counted cards from all the relatives, and, though humorless in her manner, was a mainstay of the family. She baby-sat often for Lily's daughters, though they were

nearly old enough to be baby-sitters themselves.

The girls were rapidly growing into interesting, complex individuals. Beth, once
the quiet one, was sprouting like a weed and
taking on some of the wild swagger that had
characterized Lily as a girl. Susie, for her
part, had discovered a talent for music, and
practiced the piano assiduously. There was
already talk of her attending a conservatory,
and she had become overnight a very serious and somewhat obsessive personality,
though still sweet and forthcoming to me
and to Nick. It was as though the two girls
were exchanging personalities. I marveled
at the changes time can bring to people I
thought I knew so well.

Jordan took an eager interest in all this,
charming Ingrid with compliments on her
cooking and engaging Carl in conversation
about a wide variety of technical topics.
The girls both developed an instant crush
on him. Jordan seemed to drink in the
whole France world, as though it was something he had somehow failed to savor in the
old days, something he now had to fix in

his mind and appreciate before it faded forever.

Lily thought the restoration of Brookfield was "the best thing to happen in this little backwater in a hundred years." She remembered her mother's friendship with Jordan's mother, and she felt herself a representative of Mrs. France now. She was ashamed of the town for ostracizing Elizabeth. She thought history was being set straight.

She saw the house as a monument to Jordan's family. More yet, she considered the place a monument to our childhood together, our "threeness," to which she now referred freely and affectionately to her husband. "The unholy trio, as Mom used to call us," she said.

It must have been her obvious enthusiasm for this subject, and her affection for us, that prompted Jordan to jog her memory on a tender point.

"Do you remember our promise to meet on the thirteenth tee?" he asked.

Lily seemed perplexed. "Promise? What promise?" she asked.

"The night before I left for Groton," Jordan said. "The night of the dance. You and I and Kate went out onto the golf course. We promised we would meet on the thirteenth tee in fifteen years. The Fertile Crescent. Don't you remember?"

There was a moment's silence. A colorless look, devoid of all meaning, hovered on Lily's face. Then her eyes widened in surprise.

"Oh my God!" she cried. "You're right! Of course I remember. We were lying on the grass, looking up at the moon. I still had my ball dress on, the one Kate made. Of course I remember! Oh, Jordan, how can you ever forgive me for forgetting all those wonderful times?"

And thus the memory was glossed over. Lily did not ask me whether I had remembered the rendezvous. Jordan did not even glance at me. I kept my eyes on Nick and the girls, who were playing outside the window. It was one of the strangest moments of my life. I was sure Jordan had not told Lily about meeting me that night. So she could not know what had happened, or how crucial to Jordan and me was the promise she herself had forgotten.

But the subject of Brookfield came up again. Lily, who had not seen the golf course, suggested that we take a walk around it after dinner one night. From this the idea evolved that we should belatedly carry out our rendezvous on the thirteenth tee. Jordan and I hesitated, but Lily would not take no for an answer.

"I want it to be just as it might have been if we had all remembered," she said.

We went through with our plan two nights later. We left the children home with Rob, who seemed unconcerned by his wife's nostalgic impulse. We went to the course after dinner and parked by the clubhouse.

"Oh, Jordan!" Lily exclaimed. "I can see the window where your mother used to wave to me. Remember? She was so sweet, such a sweet lady."

Jordan nodded. "The playroom is still there, where we used to have our teatime. I had it restored, with the same furniture. Do you remember the games we used to play at the table up there? Scrabble and Monopoly..."

Lily did not answer. But she took his hand, then mine.

"Let's go," she said. "I can't wait."

The sky darkened quickly as we made our way across the golf course. It was in perfect condition, the fairways smelling of cut grass from this morning's mowing. The hushed chatter of sprinklers was all around us as we walked. The contrast from the overgrown place of our youth was extreme.

"The trees," Lily said. "They're all so much older. I feel like they're watching us. Remembering us as we were. Taking us back."

We walked across fairways and down paths which seemed enchanted, because they were paths drawn in our memory as well as in the real world. Our feet seemed to know the way even before our eyes could find landmarks to orient us. It was as though the forgotten years were directing our steps.

We approached the thirteenth tee from behind, and walked up the steep hill down which we used to sled in our childhood. It took some effort, for our grown-up legs were not as springy as they had once been. Lily seemed winded, and Jordan had to take her hand and pull her along with him.

When we reached the elevated tee Lily pointed to the ocean, exclaiming, "Oh, Jordan, it's perfect. Just like the night we were here. The night we made our promise."

She turned to look at him. "You were so handsome that night at the ball," she said. "And we were still wearing our fancy clothes when we came here. Remember?"

Jordan nodded, smiling.

"Kate, do you remember?" she asked. "You met us outside. You didn't come to the ball. Oh, you should have! Shouldn't she, Jordan? We should have made you a dress, too."

But she didn't press the point. Her mind seemed to jitter from one topic to another as the memories came back.

"Wait," she said suddenly. "I want it to be just as though we all kept our promise and came separately."

Jordan and I agreed amusedly to her suggestion. We separated, retreating into the trees at different angles, and waited a couple of minutes. Then, in silence, we came out of our hiding places onto the pale glowing grass of the tee. The moon, like an accomplice to our whim, seemed to be rising out of the ocean, just as it had done so many years ago.

I saw Lily first. She came forward, looking slim and beautiful, a bit ghostly in the pale light. She took both my hands and kissed me on my cheek.

"You're the one who knew me when," she said. I could see her eyes glistening with tears.

Then we both felt Jordan's arms about our shoulders. He drew us close, and I felt our two female bodies joined by his warmth, and, much more, by his memory.

"I love you," Lily said. Then, quickly, "I love you two so much."

My hands clasped Jordan's as we both hugged her.

"Why does time have to pass?" she asked. "Why can't it belong to us forever?"

I saw my hourglass turning in my mind,

flinging every grain of human hope this way and that, skewing every memory, altering every cherished plan. How odd an accomplice time was! It changed everything beyond recognition, and yet, somehow, nothing was lost. Here we were again, brought to this moment by an inevitability that had been shadowing us all these years without our knowing it.

As I look back on that moment I can't help thinking how wrong we humans are to place all our faith in the future. Sometimes the future is as far out of reach as the stars we will never touch. But the past comes closer and closer, bringing us back the secrets which would answer all our doubts if we only knew how to listen to them.

"Promise me we'll never forget again," Lily said. "That we'll never lose each other again. I want us to be together forever."

I kissed her cheek as she had kissed mine. She could not know how completely her wish had been granted already. I hoped she would never know.

When we got home Rob and the girls greeted us with worried looks. Nick was ill.

He had fainted while the girls were teaching him a game on the back lawn.

Jordan and I hurried to the bedroom where he was lying under a sheet in the warm evening air. I touched his forehead. He seemed feverish.

"Honey, are you all right?" I held him to me and glanced at Jordan, who looked frightened.

"I'm fine," my son said. "There's nothing wrong with me. I wish everyone wouldn't get so excited."

And he did look fine. He seemed impatient more than anything else. The fear I felt found no reflection in his little eyes.

11

Life is merciful about some things. Memory, for instance. I really can't remember the course of Nick's illness. We left Summer Harbor right away and took him back to New York. The initial diagnosis was made by a physician at Mount Sinai who was a close friend of Jordan's. The blood tests left no doubt at all. The leukemia was acute. Its course would be brief.

After that an invisible screw tightened inside me. It had two effects. In the first place it annihilated all thought, except for a mindless worry about Nick that filled me like a gas. In the second place it destroyed all possibility of communication. I couldn't talk about Nick's illness, not to anyone.

For the first month I slept hardly at all; then I began to settle into the routine of it.

My hopelessness allowed me to sleep a few hours each night. I stayed at home with Nick, seeing to his needs, which were few. We played together as in the old days. I made his lunch, his snacks. I took him for his transfusions. I watched him grow weaker, and told myself each morning that he looked the same as he had the morning before.

Jordan, of course, reacted with fierce paternal concern and a determination to have everything done that could be humanly done. He took Nick to the best specialists in New York, and had consultants flown in from the Mayo Clinic and from Europe. Experimental therapies were tried until Jordan realized they were causing the boy more pain than they were worth.

Then Jordan, a realist as well as a loving father, gave up.

We couldn't move into the Rye house permanently because Nick was in the hospital too often. We had to stay in Manhattan. Jordan curtailed his own activities, usually returning from the office by two or three, and finally spending the whole day at home with Nick.

Nick helped us through it. With his hollow eyes he managed an imitation of good cheer and even of humor. He told jokes that made us laugh. He sat between us on the couch, watching TV, one hand on my leg and the other on Jordan's. He behaved, heroically, as though things were normal.

He encouraged us. He told us he was feeling better when he really wasn't. He made a show of going out to play with his friends when I could see it was too tiring for him. He agreed when I suggested his favorite snacks, including the famous popcorn recipe, even when he couldn't really keep anything down anymore. And later, when he was bedridden, he greeted me with the same old smile, rendered more poignant by illness, that said "Mom."

Jordan and I slept close together in our bed during that winter, our bodies always touching. But we never made love. During the day I often noticed that Jordan would come into the room where I was, for no discernible reason and with nothing to say.

I realized he was aware of the awful gulf between us, and was doing what little he could to remain in contact with me.

Nick understood what was going on. He seemed to see himself as the bond that held us together. He often called one of us into the room where the other was sitting or working. Later, when he was in the hospital for good, he would always ask, ''Where's Dad?'' when I came in alone. If we were both there he directed his remarks or anecdotes to both of us, forcing us to join together in our very attention to him. Oh, he was a diplomat to the end.

Then one night I was there with him alone. The room was dark. Jordan must have been on the phone down the hall, or talking to the doctor. Nick said to me in a small voice, ''This isn't fair to you.''

''What do you mean, honey?''

''You've been such a good mom,'' he said. ''And now you're so pale and thin.''

I don't remember what I responded. Something weak about being perfectly fine. But his next words ring in my memory like the tolling of my own end.

"Be good to Daddy," he said, "after I'm gone."

"Honey," I said, "I'll always be good to your father."

"But," he added, "make sure he understands how you really feel."

I was silent for a moment.

"Promise?" he insisted, watching me closely.

"I promise." I was not sure what I was promising, but I could not say no.

These words sapped me of some last remnant of strength, and when I heard the door open I told Jordan with my eyes that I had to be alone. I hurried to the ladies' room, sat in one of the stalls and sobbed for a long time, looking at my watch and trying to make myself stop.

Nick left us the next week. We buried him in Maine, where Jordan's mother was buried. Lily and Rob and the girls were there, as were the Frances. They were devastated almost beyond words. After the service we all went back to Lily's house and spent an evening whose details I can't remember.

Then Jordan and I returned to New York.

* * *

I didn't keep my promise. I couldn't talk to Jordan about Nick. I couldn't tell him "how I really felt." In the course of Nick's illness I had exhausted what was left of my belief in my relationship with Jordan, as well as my hope for anything in the world.

I shrank into myself. So did Jordan. We stayed together in the apartment; neither of us had the courage to go see the little house in Rye. It had been Nick's house, really, and we would never set foot in it again except to remove the paintings and sketches from Nick's room.

We watched the weeks pass as we went to work and came home to greet each other. We almost never touched. Occasionally one of us would reach out with a word, a look— but something rose up between us, and it was as though we were invisible to each other.

After a couple of months I couldn't take any more, and I told Jordan I was moving out. He made a show of protesting, but I could feel his surrender right away. I found a new apartment in my old neighborhood on Staten Island. He helped me move, looking incongruous and handsome in his jeans and sweatshirt. He was one of the richest men in America, but it was as though we were two struggling students, grunting as we moved tables and televisions and boxes of books into my empty rooms.

In all these years Jordan had never told me he loved me. Nor had I said the words to him. Nick was the bond between us, and Nick was gone. As I moved out I thought it would be as much a relief to Jordan as it was to me. But the look in his eyes was one of complete despair. I took that memory with me, too, and anointed it with some of my countless tears during the time that followed.

12

* * *

It is one of those November days when the sun seems as warm as September, but the air in the shade already has the chill of Christmas. I am ten years old.

Lily and I are walking toward the east side of town, our jackets in our hands. The grass is turning brown in the yards. The trees are bare, except for a few clinging leaves which display their bright colors rather forlornly, like pennants left over from a forgotten pageant.

We are not in the best of moods. We had a fight this noon, right after lunch. Lily was feeling restless and wanted to go out. I was curled up in the old armchair by the window in our room, reading a book. It is one of my favorite pastimes, sitting in that rather beat-up chair, into which I sink very deep, and seeing the bright natural light from the window fall on the pages.

"Let's go out," Lily said with a slight edge in her voice.

"Mmm," I replied noncommittally, reading my way down the right-hand page of *Pride and Prejudice*. I am in my Jane Austen period, and have already read all the novels two or three times.

"You never want to do anything," Lily said. "All you want to do is sit reading some old book. There's more to life than books, you know, Kate."

It was a deliberate jab, and I felt the sting. My absorption in books irritates Lily because she is not a great reader. Sometimes I suspect she is a bit jealous of my reading. At other times I think she is contemptuous, and right to be so.

I stuck to my guns in silence, and

she left the room. But after half an hour I got lonely and went to find her.

"All right," I said. "Where shall we go?"

"Out. Anywhere outside!"

She is still annoyed with me; I can tell by the stiff way she is walking. We turn into the narrow road that leads to Jordan's house. Both of us are hoping that Jordan will shake us out of this mood.

We knock at the kitchen door as always. Mrs. Dion, the brisk English cook, answers. She sends one of the maids to get Jordan.

As we stand in the kitchen we can hear voices in a nearby room. Mrs. Brady is speaking with one of her attorneys. She is upset. Her voice keeps rising to a shout. The attorney is trying to calm her down. The louder she talks, the more slurred are her words. She always talks a little oddly, because she takes a lot of different medications; but today her voice is strident and reckless. As Jordan enters the kitchen,

zipping up his jacket, we hear a single
obscenity echo through the walls, followed by the attorney's soothing murmur.

Jordan goes to kiss his mother goodbye. He does not invite us to greet her.
Lily and I look at each other as we
hear her muffled voice swing into the
familiar modulation of her affection
for Jordan.

"Have a good time," she calls after
him as the door opens. "Kiss the girls
for me!"

Even as his face appears in the doorway we can hear her screaming at the
attorney again. There is an undertone
of panic in her voice that often pre-
sages one of her little breakdowns. No
doubt she will be in bed for the rest of
the day.

None of us says anything as we head
across the lawn. But an unspoken
agreement turns our feet toward the
golf course. Clumps of dead leaves lie
sodden in the grass, which has not
been cut. The shutters and trim of the

house are in serious need of painting, I notice. It is as though the decay of autumn has affected the house as well as the grounds.

By the time we reach the Fertile Crescent, a thin cloud cover has obscured the sun, whose diffused light now gives everything an odd, unfriendly glare. I squint toward the ocean, which looks gray and cold.

"Let's play hide-and-seek," Lily suggests.

"There's no place to hide," I object, perhaps motivated a bit by my lingering pique against her.

"That will make it more fun. Come on!" she insists. "Who's going to be It first?"

"I will." I volunteer because I want the temporary solitude of being It, with my friends out of sight. I am feeling hemmed in and restless.

I stand against the thick trunk of one of the oaks and count to fifty, my ears alert to the vague sounds of Lily and Jordan secreting themselves. The wind from the ocean whips under my jeans, chilling my calves and ankles.

When I turn around my friends are nowhere to be seen. The fairway extends back toward the tee, the turf almost gray under the cloudy sky. For a couple of minutes I stand listening to the groan of the tree branches and the faint rustle of a leaf being blown along the grass. It is a melancholy day; the whole world seems hunched on itself against the wind.

I walk uphill along the path. I move slowly and watch the trunks of the trees. Not only is there no sign of my friends, but I can't see a decent place to hide. Autumn has stripped the woods of their cover; everything is bare.

I search for a while, becoming more lonely every minute. Then, as I am approaching the tee, I notice a pile of leaves that has collected against one of the snow fences. I move toward it slowly, my footsteps making no sound on the grass. A hint of movement among the leaves confirms my suspicion. I stop right in front of the pile and try to guess where the hider's foot is located. The pile exudes that palpable tension which every player of hide-and-seek knows. I have found my mark.

I bend slowly down and slip my hand in among the leaves. There is a rustle as someone tries to wriggle away. I dive into the pile, searching with both hands for any part of a body.

"Got you!" I cry.

To my surprise they are both in there. A jean-clad leg flails toward me; a hand grabs my ankle. Soon all three of us are writhing, laughing, as the crisp dead leaves crinkle against our cheeks and tickle our necks. I feel the firm pushing limbs of something that might be boy or girl, and smell the unique scent of young bodies touched by humus and grass and autumn. "You're It! You're It!" I shout, though I'm not sure whom I have hold of.

Faces become visible at last. Lily's long light hair is full of leaves and twigs. Jordan's collar is awry. Our struggle continues pointlessly, as though the game were merely a pretext for a more obscure contest of some kind. After a while we collapse into the pile of cold leaves, which offers us, however, a certain amount of protection against the wind.

Lily is looking up at the sky, her arm around Jordan's neck. At that moment a scattering of raindrops, blown sideways by the ocean wind, plops onto the pile of leaves. I look at Jordan's face, and see that the raindrops on his cheeks are mingling with tears that were already there.

Remembering his mother's performance back at the house, I look at Lily. She seems unaware of what I have seen; yet her arm is curled protectively around Jordan.

The sky is darkening quickly. We lie there savoring our expectation as the moment of eclipse, sun to rain, prolongs itself. I can feel my friends' breathing almost as intimately as my own. A hand touches mine. It is Jordan's. I clasp the small fingers gently.

Now the rain arrives in earnest. We get up and run to the little shelter behind the tee, which is for golfers to use when it rains. We put our coats on, because it has gotten abruptly colder.

We stand for a while, undecided as to what to do next. Then, to our surprise, the rain begins to turn to sleet. The change seems amazing, for only a half hour ago the sun seemed poised to come out and make this day as warm as May.

"It's going to snow," Lily predicts.

"No, it's not. It's too early for snow."

But Lily is right. After a while the sleet becomes lighter, more graceful, and then flakes of snow are dancing down the sky, alighting on grass and leaves and melting instantly. The branches of the empty trees are dark and glistening now. The flakes grow larger, flopping indolently in the breeze, and after a while, to our amazement, the ground begins to turn white.

"Come on," Lily commands. She runs to the middle of the tee and whirls around under the falling snow, laughing and dancing and sticking out her tongue to catch the snowflakes. We join her. We twirl until we are dizzy, and then we sit down and let the snow cover us. To me it feels as though we are in the middle of a magic globe overturned and shaken by an unseen hand to make Indian summer turn to fresh cold winter.

We are getting soaked, but we stay there, joined by our own exultation and the conspiring violence of the sky. We can't make up our minds to get up. The time and place seem bewitched. We are straddling a compressed moment of pure change, and it seems to uplift us, to free us from the world's cares. I look at Jordan. His face is wet, and snowflakes melt in his hair as I watch.

He smiles at me. His tears seem forgotten now.

We are quite a mess by the time we get back to Jordan's house. Mrs. Dion greets us with exclamations about our soaked clothes, the crazy weather and our health. "A chill like that will settle right in your bones," she says.

We girls have to take off our pants and put on some of Jordan's, which fit me all right but are comically small on Lily. A servant, summoned by the cook, has started a fire in the library, and it roars and crackles as it consumes the kindling. Mrs. Dion brings tea. We drink it thirstily and eat the large cinnamon cookies that came out of the oven an hour ago. Mrs. Dion scuttles this way and that in the other rooms, drying our clothes and shaking her head at the snow which is falling harder now, making silent little piles on the tree branches outside.

Time passes. The sky is dark now, for night is coming earlier every day at this season. The fire is burning very hot, the tea things have been removed and we three children are sitting on the rug staring into the flames. Mrs. France has been called, because Mrs. Dion doesn't want us walking home through so much snow. By the time we are picked up and taken back home it will be time for supper.

Jordan is between us, each of his hands on the upraised knee of the girl beside him. He seems at peace, though I can't tell whether he is still worrying about his mother, who has not shown her face since we came back from the golf course.

I feel very privileged as the flames dance before my tired eyes. Nature put on a great show this afternoon for our amusement. But there was more to it than that. Today three seasons rushed together and intermingled, their glory helping us to forget the battles we were too young to win. Our threeness was proven by the sky. If we stick together, nothing can ever harm us.

*   *   *

After Nick died and Jordan left I often lay awake between dreams, haunted by my memory of that day when the rain turned to snow on the Fertile Crescent. I was alone now, I had lost everything I had loved the most. The memory was like an open wound, because it evoked a time when misfortune might happen, when scars might ache, but when nothing was a match for our belief in each other and in the world that was our companion.

Too drained to cry anymore, I lay drugged by exhaustion, my childish self wide-awake inside my adult body, as though waiting in front of the fireplace for Mrs. France to arrive to take us home. My legs still felt the heat of the dying fire through my borrowed pants, and I heard the snow touching at the window with tiny muted taps like omens, calling out love and confirmation.

13

Years passed. I threw myself into my work. I found solace in writing about other people, their achievements and tragedies. I thought as little as possible about myself. The gulf inside me hardened into an icy core that held life at bay. The world around me seemed to mirror what was going on inside me. People everywhere were pulling back from their dreams and concentrating on a kind of survival in which all was not lost, though much was renounced. Little thought was given to the past; even less to the future. The whole world had a ghostlike air, grimly serious and yet not real. Like everyone else I went through the motions of living and waited for the next blow.

When it came, I was not as surprised as I thought I would be.

I should have guessed that Lily's frail-looking beauty, combined with her increasing resemblance to her mother, was concealing something dangerous.

Lily had inherited her mother's chronic heart failure years ago, and had told no one but Rob. Looking back, I realized that this explained the haunting quality of her beauty as she grew older. I also realized it was the secret behind the new tenderness I observed between her and Rob. There were still conflicts, but there was an affection between them that seemed firm and brave, just as her mother's affection for Mr. France had been. Their regret over past mistakes was pushed aside by the alliance they forged in the face of illness.

As Lily's best friend I had never quite forgiven Rob for having cheated on her, but now I felt real sympathy for him. His life-long battle with his father had been psychological as well as practical. Rob had attained financial security, but the personal cost had been high. He had never achieved the independence as a person that he had dreamed of when he first made up his mind to go to law school. He had stayed in his hometown, he had worked for his father, he had been forced to play a role in his family that he had never wanted to play. It was this frustration that led to his infidelity, I believed.

The only remarkable thing about his life, the only truly special thing, was his marriage to Lily. Because of her he was not completely defeated by the world. He seemed acutely aware of this now that she was ill.

There was a new solicitousness in him, and also a new admiration. When she came down in a dress for a dinner out or a social evening, Rob's eyes would light up. "Just look at your mother," he would say to the girls. "Isn't she beautiful?"

Of course he gave her little gifts, did more chores for her and generally fussed over her more. But it wasn't any of this that so touched me. It was the look of admiration and of terror in his eyes. He knew he was going to lose her. He knew she was going to die young.

As for Lily herself, she was now forced

to reenact her mother's last years in some significant ways. She had to spend more and more time in bed, and the girls would rush up to see her, just as Lily and I had rushed up to greet and be greeted by Mrs. France when we were girls. Sometimes I was in the room with her when they arrived, and I was astonished by my own sense of déjà vu.

"Settle down, now," she would say as Beth or Susie began reporting something about a new friend, a boy perhaps. "Tell me all about it."

Or, again, "Just look at you two!" she would compliment them when they came in. "Here I thought it was a dull and rainy day, and you bring a ray of sunshine right in my door!" That was the sort of thing Mrs. France used to say.

Her body was wraithlike now, too thin. And yet the old energy still showed through when she felt strong enough. The doctor allowed her to play tennis as long as she didn't run the court. She had to stay in one position. I was playing Canadian doubles with her and Rob one day, when Rob hit a sharp dipping shot toward the baseline. We both expected Lily to let it go, but she suddenly flung herself after it, moving just like the old Lily, and hit it sharply past me for an outright winner.

"Take that, you little bastard," she murmured, speaking not only to the ball but to her damaged body and to the fate that was destroying her. In that little moment I admired her courage more than ever.

But events like that came less and less often. Lily had always cleaned her own house, but now most of the work was too strenuous for her, and a cleaning woman had to be hired. She could take trips with the family and do all the normal things, like going to the movies, attending her daughters' recitals, going to a family gathering. But she always had to come home early, and she suffered episodes of weakness and palpitation that maddened her. Most painful of all, I think, was the sacrifice of her long walks. A solitary walk had always been her deepest method of release, of meditation. Now she substituted extra time upstairs in her studio for the walks. The outer world she had explored so recklessly as a girl was slipping away from her, soon to become a mere view from her bedroom window.

Time was passing, and with each visit to Lily I was farther away from Jordan. As Lily herself got weaker, she saw my relationship with Jordan receding into the past. And, now that I look back, I realize she must have seen the possibility of happiness growing more remote in me. I was giving up on life with my mind, as she was being forced to do by her body.

She only brought up the subject in a serious manner once. It was a year after Nick died. Jordan was in the news again, this time for his acquisition of a major New York publishing company, which was to form part of his communications conglomerate.

We had talked about it briefly over dinner. Afterward Lily and I took a walk around the neighborhood. It was summer again, and fireflies drooped and floated among the bushes on the front lawns of her street. Lily was wearing a sweater despite

the balmy evening warmth, and I noticed
how slowly she walked. In the old days I
never could keep up with her. Now I had
to slow my own stride so as not to embarrass her.

"He's only doing it because he's miserable," she said suddenly.

"Who?" I asked.

"Jordan."

There was a silence. Mixed feelings kept
me from speaking.

She pressed the point. "You were every-
thing to him," she said. "You and Nick.
He hated his life before you came along.
Now it's as though it all never happened.
As though he never knew a moment's hap-
piness. It's killing him."

"How do you know this?" I asked. "Has
he written you about it?"

My shaft went home. Lily was silent. Did
she guess that I knew about Jordan's cor-
respondence with her? If she did, she
clearly did not want to admit the truth.

"Sweetie," she said after a moment,
"when Nick died, you were the only thing
Jordan had left in the world. Losing you

destroyed him. You seemed so determined to break it off. Now he thinks the only reason you lived with him in the first place was so that Nick could have a man to love him.''

Again there was a silence. I had no answer to this logic. I was too exhausted, spiritually, to think of one.

''But it isn't true, is it?'' she asked. ''Jordan was never just a roommate to you. I could see it in your eyes, when you looked at him.''

I was silent.

''And yet,'' she said, ''you seemed to hide that look whenever he looked at you. As though you didn't want him to know how you felt.''

For some reason this speech made me very angry. I felt a flare of jealousy. It was easy for Lily to say these things. Jordan had loved her all his life, had never got her out of his heart for a single instant. The only reason he had ever taken an interest in me was that I was his only living link to her. Indeed, the only reason he had come to our rendezvous, and conceived Nick with me, was that he had hoped and expected to find her there. *Lily, is that you?* Those words had haunted my dreams all these years. I would never be able to silence them as long as I lived.

"I just can't see him," I said. "Not after Nick. I couldn't be with him again." I looked at her. "Sometimes I think the only thing keeping me going is my knowledge that I won't see Jordan again," I added.

Lily nodded sadly. I think she understood. She knew me very well, after all.

But I was not to realize how well until the end of our dream together.

It turned out that Lily's heart condition was worse than her mother's. She suffered a series of attacks, at first small ones and then bigger and bigger. Three years after Nick's death she was on her own deathbed.

I had been with her only a few weeks before, but Rob called me in New York to tell me the end was coming. He was calm about it—he had had plenty of time to get used to the idea—but there was a hopelessness in his voice that made it almost unrecognizable. He sounded like an old man.

I flew up the next day. Lily had been moved to the France house for some reason. They had set up a hospital bed for her. Ingrid was sharing the nursing duties with a special nurse Rob had hired. Carl, of all people, opened the door to us. I hurried upstairs and hesitated on the landing. Then I realized Lily was in her mother's room. It was the biggest, and had a beautiful view of Brookfield and the hills beyond. This, I knew, was why Lily had chosen to end things here.

She looked far worse than I had ever seen her before. Her cheeks were sunken, her skin almost translucent. The arm she held out to me was pathetically emaciated, the skin black-and-blue above the wrist. It was easy to see that death was not far away. I was haunted by the idea of the ironic hourglass turning, bringing back the past to torment us with it. Lily was to die just as her mother had died. I hated the symmetry of all this, the repetition. It was like a cruel joke played by a capricious god.

"Ah," she said. "You came back. Now everything will be all right."

There was a silence. I could see the effort it cost her to speak.

"Jordan is coming," she said. "It will be the three of us again."

I turned pale, but managed a smile. "The terrible trio," I said, "together again."

Rob was standing in the doorway, listening to this. I glanced up in embarrassment, but I could see that his grief left no room for jealousy. He simply wanted Lily to have whatever she wanted now.

"Kate." Her voice was lower, confidential.

"Yes, love?" I had taken her hand, and kissed it.

She changed her mind about what she had planned to say.

"Welcome home," she said.

Jordan arrived the next day. Rob must have told him the end was near. It was I who answered the door when he rang.

"Hello, Kate." His face looked the same as it had after Nick's death, drained of life, and I had the absurd thought that he might have looked like this the whole time we had been apart.

"Hello, Jordan." I kissed his cheek and hugged him in a brisk, defensive manner.

He looked at the staircase. "How is she?"

"She wants to talk to you."

At terrible times like those we lose track of the order of events. I don't remember Jordan going upstairs, or how long he was with Lily. I have an image of him standing in the kitchen with Rob, nodding as Rob explained something the doctor had said. They looked strangely natural together, the two men. If it hadn't been for the circumstances, one might have thought they were talking business together.

Then Jordan was gone somewhere, and I was summoned to speak to Lily.

"She's very weak," Rob said.

"I won't tire her," I said.

"That's not what I meant." There was something bitter and lost behind Rob's concerned look. But I was too dazed by grief to pay it any attention.

"Shall I go up, then?" I asked.

He hugged me. The grip of his arms was surprisingly hard. "Yes. Go on."

I found Lily looking weaker than ever. It had become difficult for her to speak, so I had to lean close to her.

"Kate," she said, relief in her voice.

"Yes, dear heart." I spoke to her in her mother's words, hoping to comfort her. But she did not seem at peace. Something was tormenting her.

"Kate, listen. You've got to forgive me," she said.

"Forgive you? For what?" I smiled. "All you've ever done was to make me happy. As happy as I had a right to be."

She shook her head.

"I lied to you all these years," she said. "I let you go on thinking..." Her words trailed off. "Damn this heart," she said. "I can't think."

"Take your time," I said.

"Time." Her lips curled bitterly. "You think you have forever..."

"Oh, sweetie," I said. "What's the matter? You're surrounded by people who love you. Rob, the girls, me, Jordan..."

She shook her head at the mention of Jordan's name. Had I been much cleverer than I was, I might have guessed what was coming.

"Kate, I saw you." Her eyes were open wide, fixed on me. "I was there. I saw you."

I had no idea what she was talking about. Yet I sensed that her tone was not accusation, but rather confession.

"Saw what, darling?" I asked. "What did you see?" I half believed she was delirious.

"The night of our rendezvous at the Fertile Crescent," she said. "I was there. But I got there late. By the time I arrived you and Jordan were both there."

My breath came short. I was taken completely by surprise.

"You were there," I said.

"I did forget about our promise," she added. "I forgot all those years. Until the last moment. Something reminded me. So I decided to go. I thought you might be there.

And I wanted to see Jordan. I was married, of course, but I wanted to see how he had turned out.''

She sighed. ''By the time I got there you were already—together. I can't tell you the irony of it, Kate. Here I was, watching you two from behind the scenes, just as you must have watched the night of the ball, when I danced in the dress you had made. Oh, yes—I saw the irony.''

She paused to take several deep breaths. I could see it was draining her to talk.

''I saw what he felt for you,'' she said. ''I knew he wanted you. And I knew you deserved him. You had saved that place in your heart for him, I knew all about it. How could I know you without knowing that?''

She started to say something else, but stopped herself. I waited, holding her hand.

''I was married,'' she said. ''I had children. I had never forgotten Jordan, but I had Rob. I had chosen my life. That's why I forgot, until the last minute.''

She sighed with frustration at her own weakness.

''So, at that moment,'' she went on, ''I

decided to stay in the shadows. You had each other. It was better that way. But I was selfish. I didn't have your talent for acceptance, Kate. I felt jealous. In a way I felt betrayed, though I knew that wasn't fair. So I stole away into the darkness, and I let you think he had only come there for me. I let you think he only wanted you because you reminded him of me.''

She smiled. ''You're not surprised, are you? I was the one who knew you when. Remember? I knew you would never take credit, you would never believe he wanted you for yourself. You were always an orphan. You always thought no one really wanted you.''

She studied my face, seeing my reaction to her words.

''I was a coward, Kate, and I was lonely in my own life. So I let Jordan write to me. I encouraged him, in a way. I never said anything about separating from Rob, but I let Jordan think I was—available. Spiritually available. That I still cared. I couldn't help myself. I needed something. I let Jordan's letters be that something. They made me feel special. They made me feel I was worth more than my own life. It was a dirty, selfish thing to do. I knew it would make everyone unhappy. But I did it.''

My own hand was frozen as I held hers. None of this had ever occurred to me. She was challenging the most basic assumptions of my whole life. I had never doubted that Jordan was for her and that I was the substitute. Our ''threeness'' was built that way. I was to sew the gown, and Lily was to wear it. She was his great love.

She must have read my thoughts, for she spoke again, more urgently this time.

''He never reminded me about the rendezvous, in his letters,'' she said. ''In that one way, he wanted to test me. Well, I didn't show up. And afterward, he never mentioned it. He just kept writing—the same old Jordan. But his letters changed after he met you again and saw Nick. I could feel he was hiding something. I could feel his happiness, and his attempt to conceal that happiness, so I would think he still missed me.''

She squeezed my hand. ''He didn't miss

me. Not in the old way. You and Nick had changed all that. When I finally saw you together I understood everything. It was you he wanted. You made him happy.''

Her strength was ebbing fast, but her eyes were bright.

"But I let you go on thinking he cared for me," she said. "And I let him go on thinking it, too. A woman knows when a man has her under his skin. I knew Jordan would never completely get over me. So I lived on that fact. It was my revenge on my own fate. I had made my own bed in life, but I wasn't brave enough to sleep in it. I could have told you that you really belonged to each other. I could have released him. I could have released you, too. I didn't. You've got to forgive me for that, Kate. You've got to…''

I was speechless. I felt my friend's anguish, her desperate need for forgiveness. She was right in everything she had said. She had understood us better than we understood ourselves. I tried to think of an answer to her. It was difficult. My whole heart, my whole mind, were paralyzed.

"You don't know what to say, do you?" she murmured. "You loved me too much to think me capable of a thing like this. But you see, you were so much better than me, all along, Kate. So much better inside... Jordan couldn't see it in the old days. He was blinded by youth, by love. But he saw it later, when he met you again. That's what attracted him."

"Don't say any more," I said.

She shook her head, as though fighting for concentration.

"Go back to him," she said. "He's waiting for you. He's been so miserable without you. And he's free now... You'll have more babies. Please, Kate. Make it up with him. It isn't too late."

She saw my skepticism, or perhaps my lingering belief that none of this was possible.

"When I saw you that night," she said, "I realized that fate had taken a hand in making me late. I knew it was meant to be. The two of you—not me. I was too much of a coward to accept it, but I knew it. Go to him now. Let my—let this be what brings you back together. You'll be making us all happy. All three of us.''

She tried to sit up. I started to say something, but she fell back against the pillow.

"Lily!" I cried.

Rob came into the room. The doctor was with him.

"Lily," I said again.

She said something in an almost inaudible voice. I leaned closer to her, but she lacked the strength to repeat it.

"You'd better go now," Rob said. "Wait outside."

I got up and went to the door. The doctor was bending over Lily. As I turned away the echo of her words sounded in my ear.

"Keep our promise," she had said.

I never saw Lily again.

14

I did not do what Lily asked. Her death drained me of the courage she had tried to instill in me with her last words. The weight of the past was simply too great.

I quit my job in New York. The city was too full of memories, too full of doomed hopes and deathless dreams. I traveled for a while, carrying my few earthly possessions in the back of my car. I stayed in furnished apartments, sometimes even motels. I was afraid to put down roots. I tried to stay ahead of the cold weather—for some reason I was afraid of cold. I spent the summer in the Midwest, filling my eyes with sights I had never seen as a girl. Flat cornfields, thick woods slumbering under humid mists, and the gray choppy waters of the Great Lakes. Then the prairies as I headed west, and finally the gorgeous mountains with their snowcapped peaks, silent repositories of their nation's pride.

I went on through New Mexico and Arizona to California, where I spent a few miserable months until the freeways became too much for me. Then I turned east again. I went through Texas to Louisiana, then to Florida and north to the Carolinas. For no particular reason I came to a halt in a small North Carolina coast town where I rented a little apartment. I started working again—an essay on Southern novelists since the sixties—and counted my money. After a year I bought a little house with a view of the bay. I finished my essay and started another.

I felt very calm. A peculiar glow, cold and warm like dry ice, sustained me. My surroundings seemed reassuringly foreign. Neighbors spoke with a hospitable accent that accepted me while reminding me that I did not belong. People got used to seeing me buying gas and groceries in the town. I was a foreign object for which they had made room.

It was one of those neighbors, a young divorced woman with a little daughter, who found me the day I got sick. I woke up one morning, put on my pot of coffee, turned on my computer and collapsed halfway to the bathroom. As luck would have it, my neighbor came to the door to borrow something and saw me lying on the floor. She called an ambulance, and I was taken to the emergency room. For a day or so I hovered near death. Then I stabilized. Luckily for me, I was aware of none of this. I woke up in a pleasant little room in the Intensive Care Unit, wondering whether my coffee had finished perking.

When I realized I wasn't at home, I had a moment's confusion, the kind that makes you unsure, not only of where you are but of what year it is. At first I thought I was a girl again, back in Maine. I half expected to hear the voice of Lily's mother calling to me to get up. Outside the window was a tiny church with a cemetery alongside it. From where I lay I could see that the gravestones were weathered by the sea air almost to the point of illegibility.

My dislocation grew more profound when I saw Jordan Brady sitting in the chair at the end of my bed, looking at me.

He stood up and came to my side.

"How are you feeling?" he asked.

At first I couldn't think of a thing to say.

"What are you doing here?" I asked. And only then, "Where am I?"

Jordan smiled.

"You passed out and your neighbor found you. Acute peritonitis. For a while they thought you weren't going to make it." He took my hand and squeezed it. "But you're out of the woods now. You're going to be fine."

I blinked, trying to take all this in.

"They found my name in your address book," he said. "They thought I might be something along the lines of a next of kin. I flew right down."

"You shouldn't have," I said weakly.

"It's ironic, isn't it?" he smiled. "Both of us are orphans. When you come right down to it, I may actually be the closest thing you have to a next of kin."

I was touched by this observation. Mr. and Mrs. France were dead. My own relatives were long gone. I supposed that Ingrid, with her family feeling, would have been willing to bury me. But Jordan—yes,

Jordan in a way was next of kin to me. I had lived with him for years. I had borne his son. No one else was closer.

I looked out the window at the graves. They made a somewhat funereal view for a patient in a hospital; yet they seemed peaceful. They spoke of belonging and of a time beyond the cares of everyday living.

"What will happen now?" I asked.

"You'll be out of here in less than a week," he said. "The infection is under control. You're tougher than you look—I told the doctor that. You can go back to work as soon as you're home."

"Home?"

He nodded. "I saw your place. Your neighbor showed me. It's nice. Warm."

I felt a pang at this choice of words. Our little house in Rye, so small and intimate when we lived there with Nick, had been "warm." That was Jordan's word for it. Uncomfortably I wondered whether I had been trying to bring back the past in buying it.

"You have a nice view of the ocean," he added.

I nodded.

"Does it remind you of anything?" he asked.

Amazingly, it was only at this instant that the truth occurred to me. Until now I had felt I was living at the ends of the earth.

"Lily's house," I said. "The back windows. We could see the ocean."

"And my house," Jordan said.

There was a silence. He sat back down in the chair. I couldn't help noticing how handsome he was. There was a touch of gray at his temples now, and his face was lined. He looked deeper somehow, as though a whole additional life had been joined to his first one.

I lay looking up at the unfamiliar ceiling. I could hardly move. I felt drained by illness and by memory.

"You always did like things the way you wanted them," Jordan said. "When we were small I thought of Lily as the strong-willed one. But it was really you."

This struck me as odd. "Why do you say that?" I asked.

"Remember the night of the ball, before I left for Groton?" Jordan said. "You didn't come to the party. You sent Lily instead. She told me how hard she and her mother had tried to make you come. But you refused. You were willful, all right.''

I had never thought of that night in this way before. But now I could see that there had been a great stubbornness in me. A match for Lily's, even.

''I'll never forget dancing with her,'' Jordan said, ''knowing you had made the dress she was wearing—and knowing you were out there in the darkness somewhere, watching us. It was the strangest feeling I had ever had.''

''Why strange?'' I asked.

''You two were all I had in the world— except my mother,'' he said. ''I thought that was to be our night. The three of us. But you wouldn't come. You stayed away.'' He thought for a moment. ''It was as though you were giving her to me. Making her look as beautiful as possible, and asking me to take her.''

I said nothing. At the time it had seemed only natural to me to efface myself and send Lily to the ball. I pushed Lily forward because I didn't think myself worthy. My decision seemed self-evident. But now, looking at that night through Jordan's eyes, it did not seem so simple.

"And I felt it later, on the golf course," Jordan said. "Even though it was the three of us, I could feel that you wanted me to love her. That she was the one reserved for me. I felt it even in our promise. You were giving her to me, or trying to."

"That wasn't how I saw it," I objected weakly.

"You pulled back," he insisted.

I saw he was right. On that long-ago night, even in the heart of our "threeness," I had pushed Lily forward with all my might, because I was so sure that Jordan could not love me. And he must have felt that withdrawal on my part.

But what choice did I have? I had to remain in the shadows. That was the meaning of our mystic triangle, in my own eyes. In a way it was my only chance of believing in myself, of reaching out for happiness— through Lily.

The silence between us deepened. I lay inside my weakened body on the hospital bed, with Jordan just out of my sight. I didn't want to look at him, but I dared to warm myself with my knowledge that he was there.

"You know," he said, "before Nick died he made me promise to tell you how I really felt about you."

"Don't." My eyes filled with tears. His words devastated me. They were the same words Nick had said to me.

I fought back the sob in my throat. I stared willfully at the ceiling, on which the shadow of the curtains danced like a ghost. I could feel the graves outside the window, humbly bestowing their silent stones to the sky.

"Lily was always lighter than air," he said. "She was so perfect, she wasn't quite real. That made me want her, but not really in the way a man wants a woman. It was like recapturing a dream or a memory. Do you see?"

I was silent.

"And you—you were so human, so much like me… My heart went out to you. I loved your imperfections. Your freckles, your worried look, the way you dropped things and stumbled over words… I couldn't get enough of you." He smiled. "I

can still see the two of you coming toward
me. She was always walking ahead, faster,
with those long legs of hers. And you hung
back, a little shy, your hair in your eyes—
do you remember?''

I nodded, seeing my childish self through
the eyes of his memory.

''I loved you for the way you hung
back,'' he said. ''For the way you hid in
her shadow. She made me want to step back
and admire her from a distance. But I
wanted to take you in, to hold you close.
And you never let me.''

I sighed. How he had misunderstood me!
Or was it a misunderstanding? In my own
way I was trying to love him, trying to tell
him I loved him. I could only do it by giving him to someone else, by forcing someone else on him. That was the craziness of
my own love. How could he fail to feel that,
and thus, in a way, to give up on me?

''But you wrote to her all those years,''
I said. ''You must have loved her.''

''I did, in a way,'' he said. ''It was
like…like an old promise that had to be
kept. But the promise was made to you,
Kate, more than to her.''

He paused, as though hesitating to reveal a secret he had kept from me.

"I never told her about the rendezvous, you know," he said.

Hearing this, I remembered Lily telling me that very thing. Jordan had tested her, and she had not remembered. Or rather, she had remembered too late. And her lateness had been the key to all that followed.

"When I found you afterward, and found Nick," he said, "it was like a dream come true. No, that's not what I mean. It was like waking up from an old dream, and entering the real world at last. You did that for me, Kate. You and Nick. You brought me to life."

I was silent. I felt my own dreams contending stubbornly with the reality he described. Had I ever come back to earth in my own life? Had I ever come out of my private cloud?

"Later," he said, "I kept writing to Lily, but it was out of obligation. I knew how hard her life was. I wanted her to feel she had something more. But also, in a way, I was trying to get her approval of us being together. I told her all about you, and about

Nick. And she was generous, Kate. She loved our happiness. She told me so. She felt that, in a small way, she was part of it.'' He thought for a moment. "Do you see? By that time she was the one on the sidelines, the one watching us.''

His words paralyzed me. In so many ways history had repeated itself in our lives. But always with the actors changing places. A strange, cosmic game of musical chairs.

"I loved you,'' he said, his voice deliberate. "If only I had loved myself a little bit more... Enough to let you love me. But the world can make it difficult for a certain kind of person to do that. To dare that.''

My breath came short. He had almost literally taken the words from my own mouth. It was my truth he had spoken, but about himself.

"You were too much like me,'' I said. "You were an orphan, alone in the world. People like us have trouble believing in happiness.''

He stood up and moved to my side. He seemed relieved.

"We loved each other the best way we could, all those years. Is it ever really any different for anyone? One loves the best way one knows how.''

He took my hand. I tried one last time to hold back.

"And now it's all over, isn't it?" he asked.

I breathed deeply. I knew the warmth of those fingers better than any other human touch. "Yes. It's all over," I said.

Jordan was smiling. "You'll be out of here soon," he said. "I'll take you home."

Tears were in my eyes. "Will you?"

"Someone's got to keep an eye on you," he said.

He bent to kiss my lips. I closed my eyes. His kiss was so familiar and yet so foreign after all this time. I could feel the hourglass of my years being turned over again. Not suddenly and cruelly, like a child's impulsive game—but gently, as though by a maturer hand, to set things right. All the rivers of sand were now flowing in one direction only.

A bird flew suddenly across the sky outside the window. Still holding my hand, Jordan turned to look.

"Flying south," he said. "Where do you suppose he's coming from?"

I said nothing. All I had seen was a streak against the blue.

"A long way away, I'll bet," Jordan said. "In a hurry, too." He looked at me. "Do you suppose he'll remember where he started from when he comes to rest?"

"I don't know, Jordan."

He smiled.

"He'll have to. How else will he get back to where he's going?"

I nodded. Jordan's words were strange, but I understood them perfectly. I had wandered far in my life, but my flight from myself had always led back to the place I had foolishly forgotten.

Now two more birds, flying side by side, soared past in the wake of their leader, above the trees. I thought I saw one of them hang back for a fleeting instant, as though a bit unsure whether to see the trip through to its end, or perhaps held back by an old memory. Then it caught up, and they were gone, their cries echoing beyond the graves.

ELIZABETH GAGE

When Dusty brings home her young
fiancé, he is everything her mother
Rebecca Lowell could wish for her
daughter, and for herself...

The Lowell family's descent into
darkness begins with one bold act,
one sin committed in an otherwise
blameless life.

This time there's no absolution in...

Confession

EVA RUTLAND

NO CRYSTAL STAIR

Ann Elizabeth Carter grew up in the segregated
Atlanta of the 1920's and 1930's, part of the
privileged class. She was a charming, confident
young woman with a well-planned life ahead of her.

Then she upset all those
plans and fell in love. For
the first time she left her
sheltered life in Atlanta
to marry Rob. For the
first time she had to learn
what it really meant to be
a black woman in
twentieth-century America.

You have to guard the love
you find—and overcome the hate that finds you.

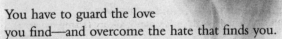

FREE

2 BOOKS

PLUS A SURPRISE GIFT!

To thank you for choosing to read this Best of the Best™ novel from MIRA® Books, we would like to send you another two books and a Mystery Gift—FREE—with NO COST and NO OBLIGATION! Simply fill in the coupon and return it to us at the address below.

And as a further thank-you we'd like to make you a bonus offer: Each month you can receive THREE of these great novels FOR THE PRICE OF JUST TWO! These books will be delivered direct to your door each month—and we'll even pay the postage and packing.

REPLY TODAY - NO STAMP NEEDED!

YES! Please send me my 2 free Best of the Best novels and Mystery Gift. If having received my free books and Gift, I do not wish to receive any more I will let you know. Otherwise each month, I will receive 3 Best of the Best novels for just £11.98— saving me a massive 33% on the combined cover prices! Even postage and packing is free! I understand that I may cancel at any time with no further obligation. I am over 18.

B0ZEC

Ms/Mrs/Miss/Mr ....Initials ....
                                                    BLOCK CAPITALS PLEASE

Surname ....

Address ....

....

....Postcode...................................

Send coupon to:
UK: FREEPOST CN81, Croydon, CR9 3WZ
EIRE: PO Box 4546, Kilcock, County Kildare (stamp required)

MIRA®